"Come away with me."

The offer, roughened by the lust tearing at him, hovered between them.

Her lips parted, moved, but nothing emerged. Anticipation and the need to press for an answer whipped inside him like a gathering summer storm, but he held back. Granting her space and time to come to her decision. Because it had to be hers, freely given.

Finally, she lifted her head, met his gaze. Desire still simmered in her eyes, as did the doubt. But so did resolve. He had his answer even before she murmured "yes."

Ross exhaled. "Good," he said. "Call me when you're about to leave work. I'll come by to pick up you and Ben tonight."

"Okay." Charlotte sighed. Then whispered, "I hope we're not making a mistake, Ross."

The assurance that they were doing the right thing hovered on his tongue, but he couldn't utter it. Because it would be a lie.

He didn't know.

And right now, he didn't care.

* * *

Back in the Texan's Bed by Naima Simone is part of the Texas Cattleman's Club: Heir Apparent series.

Dear Reader,

It's February and the month of love. Sigh. So what better time of the year to launch a new Texas Cattleman's Club series? I'm super excited about Heir Apparent! It has everything this longtime-running and wonderful series is known for—intrigue, drama, family and, of course, passionate romance.

Back in the Texan's Bed is a second-chance, secret-baby story, and whew boy! You guys are my guinea pigs! This is my first secret-baby book—can you believe it? I can't. I love to read them but have never written one before! And I had a ball writing Ross Edmond and Charlotte Jarrett's journey back to each other. They have a history that's complicated by her once being his family's employee, his father's machinations and now, a son Ross didn't know existed. Both have their guards so high, it's a wonder they can learn to trust and love again. Spoiler alert: they do. But them getting there is all the swoony fun! I hope you fall in love with Ross and Charlotte and root for their happily-ever-after!

Happy reading!

Naima

NAIMA SIMONE

BACK IN THE TEXAN'S BED

Special thanks and acknowledgment are given to Naima Simone for her contribution to the Texas Cattleman's Club: Heir Apparent miniseries.

HARLEQUIN®
DESIRE™

Recycling programs for this product may not exist in your area.

ISBN-13: 978-1-335-23270-0

Back in the Texan's Bed

Copyright © 2021 by Harlequin Books S.A.

This edition published by arrangement with Harlequin Books S.A.

For questions and comments about the quality of this book, please contact us at CustomerService@Harlequin.com.

Harlequin Enterprises ULC
22 Adelaide St. West, 40th Floor
Toronto, Ontario M5H 4E3, Canada
www.Harlequin.com

Printed in U.S.A.

Books by Naima Simone

Harlequin Desire

Texas Cattleman's Club: Heir Apparent

Back in the Texan's Bed

Blackout Billionaires

The Billionaire's Bargain
Black Tie Billionaire
Blame It on the Billionaire

Dynasties: Seven Sins

Ruthless Pride

Texas Cattleman's Club: Rags to Riches

Trust Fund Fiancé

To Gary. 143.

Prologue

Love.

Russell "Ross" Edmond Jr. sipped his scotch, relishing the smoky flavor with hints of caramel, fruit and a bite of salt, while staring out the window of the Texas Cattleman's Club meeting room at the beautiful couple currently wrapped around each other in a passionate embrace.

Ezekiel Holloway and Reagan Sinclair—Reagan Holloway now—had caused quite a scandal in Royal, Texas, some months ago when they'd eloped to Vegas against her family's wishes. Especially since Zeke's own family had been embroiled in a dirty criminal investigation that involved embezzlement and drug smuggling. But that had all been cleared up, their reputation restored, and now the newlyweds were living out their happily-ever-after.

Ross barely contained a derisive snort. Sure, the two appeared enamored and, yes, happy. The married couple kissed as if Ezekiel was heading off to sea for a months-long absence. Ross would say they were in love. Or, at least, they believed they were.

Unfortunately—or fortunately, in his opinion—he wasn't a devout disciple at the altar of the emotion that seemed like a convenient excuse for people to lose control, validate idiotic behavior or justify satisfying any impulsive desire.

What *did* he believe in?

Raising his glass to his mouth again, he turned from the view of the couple and surveyed the elegantly appointed room. Due to recent renovations at the Club, the design was less dark wood and stone, and now boasted brighter colors, larger windows and higher ceilings. Yes, the hunting trophies and historical artifacts still adorned the walls, and the stables remained, as did the pool and tennis courts. Yet, now the Club had a day care and sported painted murals, as well. The whole effect exuded a warmth that had been missing before.

But it all still conveyed wealth. Influence. Exclusivity.

And those ideals he trusted.

Money and power. They could be counted, measured, handled, manipulated, if need be, and were unfailingly consistent.

They'd never let him down.

Unlike people. Unlike *love*.

Hell, he couldn't even keep the sneer out of his inner voice.

"Ross, get over here," Russell Edmond Sr. boomed as if Ross stood farther out in the club's entryway instead of just several feet away from him. "Do that brooding shit on your own time. We have business to attend to."

Rusty. Oil mogul. Texas Cattleman's Club member. Tycoon. All things people called Russell Edmond Sr. Whereas Ross considered him *brilliant, ruthless, domineering.* And, on occasion, *manipulative bastard.*

They all fit.

With his tall, wide-shouldered and athletic build that had only gone a little soft around the middle, dark hair dusted with silver at the temples and intelligent, scalpel-sharp gray eyes, Rusty still possessed a powerful physique and commanded respect. Ross strode over to the long, cedar conference table, his gaze fixed not on his father but on the thin stack of documents in the middle of the table. His heart thumped against his sternum in anticipation. To others, those ordinary sheets of paper might seem innocuous. But to him?

Independence. Autonomy.

Identity.

Yes, this deal included the financial and marketing backing of The Edmond Organization, but this project—the luxury food, art and wine festival called Soiree on the Bay, which was to be held on a small, private island—was his baby. Well, more aptly, it was a baby that belonged to him, his siblings, Gina and Asher, and his best friend, Billy Holmes. But for the first time, he wasn't a figurehead wearing the Edmond name and the ineffectual title of executive. Wasn't a puppet tasked with carrying out Rusty-given orders. Wasn't just the useless playboy son riding the coattails of his daddy's success and reputation.

With this project, this event, he would finally step

out from under his father's shadow and show everyone he hadn't just inherited the Edmond name—he'd *earned* it. Ross would play an integral role in raising the bar, in solidifying and expanding their legacy as he elevated The Edmond Organization from the national stage to the international one. Something even Rusty hadn't managed to do in the company's history.

But Ross would.

And in the process, maybe earn that thing that had eluded him the entire twenty-eight years he'd been Rusty's son—approval.

Again, not love. Men like his father believed in that emotion even less than Ross did. Just ask Rusty's four ex-wives.

Just ask his children.

"So this is it? The final contract?" Ross set his tumbler down on the table, trying not to stare down at the documents as if they were the Holy Grail and he a Texas version of Indiana Jones.

"This is it," Billy Holmes, his college friend and future business partner, said, grinning. "The last step before Soiree on the Bay moves from dreams to reality."

"Dreams," Rusty scoffed. "Dreams are for men who don't have the balls to get out there and pursue what they want."

Ross glanced at his sister, Gina, across the table, arching an eyebrow in her direction. She rolled her eyes, but he noted the ever-present frustration there. Even this throwaway comment reflected Rusty's dismissal of women, especially in regard to business and autonomy. All because they'd had the misfortune of being born with a uterus instead of a penis. Though Gina had become as adept as Ross at masking her emotions, he caught the aggravation in her eyes. The hurt.

"Fortunately, everyone in this room is well equipped with their balls," Billy drawled, slanting a grin at Ross's baby sister. "Except for you, Gina. And thank God for it." His gentle teasing garnered the desired effect, and the shadows in her eyes dimmed, lightening with humor and gratitude. "And once we all sign, no one will ever question the influence and reach of The Edmond Organization."

Rusty grunted and slid the contract over the table toward him. As he scanned through, Billy glanced at Ross and winked. Ross smothered a snort, shaking his head. His pal had been a charmer in college, and since he arrived in Royal two years ago, he hadn't changed a bit. With his impeccable appearance and manners, generosity with his time, acumen and money, Billy had everyone from business associates to the often clique-ish members of Royal society wrapped around his finger.

Including Rusty, which was a feat unto itself.

The older man had even vouched for Billy with the Texas Cattleman's Club, and Ross's friend had scored a much-coveted membership. Billy shared a camaraderie and closeness with Rusty Edmond that even his kids couldn't claim.

But that was Billy. The Billionaire Whisperer, they jokingly called him.

All right, maybe not so jokingly.

"This looks good," Rusty announced, reaching inside his suit coat to remove a thick gold pen. With flourish, he signed his name on the designated line. "You did good, son," he praised Billy.

Picking up his drink, Ross sipped, waiting for the dark slick of jealousy to slide down his throat to his chest along with the liquor. After all, his father had just called another man *son*, and Ross was human. So yes, pinpricks of jealousy did sting him. But relief reigned as the most prevalent emotion.

And if that wasn't a fucked-up indictment on the Edmond family dynamic, he didn't know what was.

But one quick glance at Gina and at Asher, his stepbrother whom Rusty had adopted after marrying Asher's mother—wife number two—verified he wasn't alone in this sentiment. That same relief shone his siblings' gazes, as well. Anytime Rusty leashed in that infamous mercurial temper was a reason to breathe deep and bask in the peaceful, and probably brief, moment.

A knock on the door reverberated in the room, and Billy waved toward the contract. "That's my surprise. I'll get that while you finish up here."

Ross moved forward first, adding his signature to the contract, followed swiftly by Gina and Asher. By the time they all finished, Billy returned, bearing a silver tray laden with a bottle of champagne and five glass flutes. In moments, Billy had the sparkling wine poured and they'd all lifted their glasses to meet high over the table.

"A toast." Billy paused, blue eyes gleaming. "To The Edmond Organization stamping its indelible brand on not just the US, but the world. I think we've all waited for this day to arrive. So, to achieving long-awaited goals. And finally, to all of you, the Edmond family. May you all get what you so richly deserve." He smiled. "Emphasis on the rich."

They clinked glasses and sipped the champagne, celebrating this deal that they'd all put so much time into bringing to fruition.

"Vendors have already been contacting me about the festival, just from rumors alone. They want in. I predict tickets will sell out within hours of going on sale," Asher said. "Soiree on the Bay is going to be wildly successful. For all of us."

"It needs to be," Ross added gruffly. "This is the inaugural launch. The potential to make this a coveted, exclusive and profitable annual event is huge. So the first one needs to go off without a hitch. Besides, vendors and investors are pouring money in with ours, and the charities that will benefit from this are counting on it. On *us*."

"We'll do it," Gina swore, her tone firm. "I have zero doubts about that."

"With the Edmond reputation and money on the line, hell yes, you'll make this a success. You have no choice. I want people talking about this festival for months before and after."

"Oh, they will. Rest assured, Rusty, they will," Billy murmured, a corner of his mouth lifting in a half smile. "I promise you. This will be an event that no one will ever forget."

Once more, excitement stirred in Ross's gut. In just months, vendors, investors, the press and ticketholders would flock to *their* festival. He sipped from the bubbly wine, savoring the light flavor with a smile. It would be business for him, but not *all* business. People from all over the world would be visiting the private island where the event would be held. Which meant hordes of beautiful women. Most specifically, women who wouldn't expect more from him than the temporary, mutually agreed upon use of each other's bodies for the hottest, dirtiest pleasure.

He knew the reputation he'd earned—they called him a playboy. And admittedly, it was a moniker he deserved. Flings, one-night stands—the filthy hot fun without the messy emotional attachments that could wrap around a man, trap him, strangle him until he couldn't think, couldn't function, couldn't fucking *breathe*.

His chest tightened, a vise slowly turning until he could practically hear his ribs creak in protest. A face, faded and nebulous, wavered across his mind's eye like a mirage a dying man glimpsed seconds before his heart and body surrendered. Ross's grip tautened around the glass, his jaw clenching. He wasn't a dying man, but he'd beat the shit out of himself if he ever allowed himself to be that humiliatingly *weak* again. To allow himself to believe fucking was more than that—two people satisfying an itch before going their separate ways. It didn't have anything to do with emotion…with love.

God, why in the hell did that word keep rebounding in his head today?

He mentally shook his head, dislodging the wayward thoughts—and that damn face—from his head. Focus. He needed to focus.

He and his siblings hovered on the precipice of obtaining their individual and collective purposes. Of achieving those *goals* that Billy had toasted about mere moments ago.

And nothing would stand in their way.

One

"Charlotte, can I borrow you for a moment?"

Charlotte Jarrett looked up from plating and double-checking the dishes before sending them out for customers to dine on. This was her kitchen, her baby. And her recipes were her soul. If the food wasn't flawless, she sent it back for another plate to be prepared. Nothing less than perfection went out of here.

"Sure thing," she said to Faith Grisham, the manager of Sheen, the restaurant where Charlotte had been working as head chef for two weeks now. "Give me just a couple of minutes to finish up here and get these out and served."

Faith, a beautiful, no-nonsense woman who could've passed for actress Zoe Saldana's younger sister, nodded with a flick of her fingers. "Of course." Number one rule in this kitchen: the food came first, because the customer did. And though Sheen enjoyed popularity and success, they couldn't afford to become lax. One negative review, one bad write-up, and their status as Royal's newest favorite could quickly spin the other way. Nobody wanted that.

Least of all Charlotte.

Not when she'd sacrificed everything to return to the hometown she'd had no intention of ever stepping foot in again.

Not when she had so much riding on this.

Like expanding her clientele to include more exclusive and influential connections. A possible owning partnership in Sheen. Growing her reputation, to take one more step toward becoming a world-renowned chef. Earning her Michelin stars.

And most important, providing a stable, financially secure future for herself and Ben.

Even as she executed the finishing touches on her signature dish of braised beef over Thai noodles with seared tomatoes and asparagus, that warm rush of joy that only thoughts of her beautiful little boy could conjure slid through her like melted sunshine. He'd saved her, blessed her with a reason to keep pushing forward, instead of lying down and fading away. He was her *everything*, so it seemed only fair that she would be more than willing to give up everything to ensure he had a well-rounded, happy and full life.

Even if it meant swallowing her pride and being the one to try to bridge the divide that had estranged her from her parents after she'd left Royal.

Even if it meant facing the memories—and demons—that continued to plague her three years later.

Smothering a sigh, she refocused on the task at hand. Satisfied that the meals were ready, she quickly cleaned the edge of the plates with a paper towel soaked with white vinegar, then set them on the custom-built warming shelves for servers to come pick up.

"Rachel," Charlotte called to her sous-chef, "fire those plantain burgers. They're up next."

"Yes, Chef, on three," the older woman immediately replied, informing Charlotte that the Kobe beef burger, set between two slices of fried plantain, would be ready for her to plate with her made-from-scratch avocado ranch dressing in three minutes' time.

Wiping her hands on a towel, Charlotte turned to Faith, smiling as the manager typed out a message so fast on her ever-present phone that her thumbs blurred.

"What'd you need?" Charlotte asked.

"You, your effervescent personality and beautiful face."

"Do you want me to clue you in on how pimp-ish that sounds, or are we just going to ignore it?" Charlotte drawled, quirking an eyebrow.

"Ignore it."

Charlotte snickered, then grinned. As she had been headhunted from the California restaurant where she'd been working, so had Faith, from her native San Antonio, to run Sheen.

Faith had created a name for herself as a Jon Taffer in heels. Not that Sheen had been failing and needed rescuing when Faith had been brought on several weeks ago and prior to Charlotte's hiring, but the owners had wanted to make sure their venture hit the ground running from the beginning.

"Okay, give. I have nearly a full restaurant of hungry customers to feed," Charlotte said, crossing her arms. "What's up?"

"What's up is I just heard from a source who shall remain nameless that the food critic from the *New York Voice* magazine will be dropping by Sheen next Tuesday."

Astonishment vibrated through Charlotte, and she rocked back on her nonskid sugar skulls clogs. "What?" she whispered excitedly. "You're *kidding* me!"

The *New York Voice.* Holy… The alternative e-zine had only been around for the last five years, but it had immediately become popular not just within New York, but nationally and internationally, too. With its hard-hitting investigative journalism stories on societal issues, along with its focus on the cultural community of art, music, literature and food, it had already won the National Press Foundation Award as well as the George Polk Award. For Sheen to receive a positive review in their food column would be amazing publicity not only for the restaurant, but also for Charlotte's career.

"Nope, all true. Which means we need to be at our very best next Tuesday. I'll handle the front of the house and make sure it's super clean, all the servers are on point. And you're responsible for the back. I don't think I need to explain what a rave review could do for us."

"You don't." Charlotte shook her head, grinning. "And believe me, we will be better than perfect."

"I know it," Faith said, and for several moments they

stood there, grinning at each other like two giddy fools. "We got this," she whispered.

"Oh, we *so* got this," Charlotte whispered back, the excitement still humming inside her joined by a steely resolve.

Yes, a glowing write-up and recommendation would mean great things for Sheen, but it went deeper than that. This restaurant was managed by a black woman. The kitchen was run by a black woman. The staff were women of various ethnicities—but they were all women. When the owner had come up with the concept, maybe it'd been a gimmick to differentiate Sheen from the other new restaurants popping up. But both Charlotte and Faith had vowed that they wouldn't let it remain some publicity ploy. Their restaurant would be one of the most successful establishments known for its sublime service and outstanding food. And so far, they were succeeding at this aim.

"Chef, your presence has been requested at one of the tables. They asked to meet you," Carlie, one of their servers, interrupted.

"Thanks, Carlie." Charlotte nodded at the younger woman. "I'd better get out there," she said to Faith, trying to conceal a grimace.

But apparently, she hadn't been quick or stealthy enough. A smirk curled the other woman's mouth.

"Part of the job, Charlotte," she reminded her.

"I know, I know," Charlotte muttered, unsnapping her baggy white executive chef coat and shrugging out of it, revealing the large T-shirt underneath. She strode over to the hooks near the door that led out of the glass-enclosed kitchen and removed her more formal and fitted turquoise chef coat with three-quarter-length sleeves, black piping and fabric-covered buttons. "It's not that I don't like going tableside," she grumbled, slipping into the coat and quickly fastening it over her chest. "I'd just much rather be cooking. I always feel like I'm on display."

"Well, get used to it. You're not naive enough to not know that these days it's as much about the chef as the food. That face and pinup body is an asset along with your truffle mac 'n' cheese." Faith's matter-of-fact tone stole a bit of the wind out of Charlotte's imminent tirade about the unfairness of her appearance being a factor at all. Mostly because, as unreasonable as it might be, Faith was correct.

It still annoyed her, though.

"Thank you for those words, oh, wise one," Charlotte drawled. Then, turning to Carlie, she smiled. "Lead the way."

As they exited the kitchen, Charlotte couldn't help surveying the restaurant, where she spent nearly as much time at as the home she rented for her and Ben. A sister site to The Bellamy's Glass House restaurant, Sheen was made entirely out of glass. This evening, the low lighting complemented rather than competed with the setting sun's rays that poured through the ceiling-to-floor windows, bathing the tables and patrons in its orange-and-red glow.

Beautiful.

And one day, hopefully, hers. Well, partly.

Carlie led her through the restaurant toward the far corner that boasted one of the best tables because of its gorgeous view of Royal. The table, which sat on a small dais, overlooked the entire restaurant. Which meant one thing—VIP guest.

Charlotte fixed a polite smile to her face as she neared the table. Five minutes, max, then she had to return to—

Oh, God.

Frigid fingers of shock crackled through her veins, and her feet stuttered to a stop. Startled stares swept over her like ants marching over a picnic blanket, prickling her skin. But she couldn't move. Couldn't jerk her gaze away from a pair of icy blue eyes.

Her heart attempted to drill a hole through her rib cage, each beat pumping pain and fear to every artery and organ. Pain, fear and something so much more complicated.

Pain, because for the first time in three years she stared into the beautiful, cold face of the man she'd once loved. A man who had been willing to take her body but not her heart.

The convoluted emotion was a noxious mixture of anger, resentment and—Jesus, she hated herself for this—a residue of the delight that just a glimpse of him used to stir within her.

And fear… Damn, the *fear*, because she wasn't just coming face-to-face with Russell Edmond Jr., the man who'd broken her heart.

She was coming face-to-face with her son's father.

A son he had no idea existed.

Two

Fuck no.

Ross stared at a ghost from his past.

A ghost that, as much as he'd tried to banish with time, work and other women—sometimes alcohol—he'd failed to exorcise.

Charlotte Jarrett.

Former head chef at his family's ranch. Ex-lover. The woman who'd walked away uncaring of the damage she'd left behind.

Another woman who'd abandoned him without a backward glance.

Ice coated his skin, sinking deeper, seeming to freeze the very marrow of his bones.

He hated seeing her again. Hated that she hadn't changed. Hated that her tall, graceful frame still boasted the same gorgeous, deadly curves that his hands could trace from muscle memory. That she remained as beautiful as ever—silken, hickory-brown skin, oval-shaped eyes framed by a thick fringe of dark lashes, regal cheekbones with slightly hollowed cheeks, an elegantly sloped nose and...

He transferred his hands to his thighs so the white tablecloth hid his clenched fists.

And a mouth that should be slapped with an indecency citation. Those plush lips were so flagrantly sensual he dared any man to glance at them and not imagine them dragging him willingly to the edge of ecstasy. An edge he'd hovered and plummeted over many times with her...

He hated that his cock had hardened the instant his eyes clashed with that startled, wide, espresso gaze. Most of all, he despised the heavy, primal thud of his heart that echoed in his stiffening flesh.

What the hell was Charlotte doing back in Royal?

She'd left him. Discarded him like trash. As if she'd never taken him inside her. Or moaned his name in that sexy whimper he'd become addicted to eliciting from her. As if they'd never curled their sweat-dampened bodies around each other, wrapped in their own private cocoon where the outside world couldn't intrude.

Charlotte Jarrett had completed the lesson Ross's mother had started; he'd earned a well-learned and hard-won degree in the field of emotional desertion. *Be foolish enough to become attached, and they don't stay.* Maybe it was something in him that made it so easy for them to walk away from—his father's four marriages were exhibits A through D. Rusty went through women as often as the change of guard took place at Buckingham Palace. Like father, like son. At least Ross didn't marry them.

No, he'd finally learned, courtesy of Charlotte. Fuck and move on to the next one. No promises. No strings. No entanglements. No feelings. As long as he adhered to those rules, no one would ever play him for a fool again.

Never hurt me. Never leave me.

With a sharp mental slash, Ross incised those ridiculous and too weak words from his head. He hadn't been hurt when Charlotte had up and left Royal. Left *him*. He'd been mad as hell. And that anger continued to simmer inside his chest, kindling lower in his stomach as she neared the table where he and Billy dined.

If he'd known that when his friend requested to meet Sheen's chef he would be confronting Charlotte again, Ross would've stalked right out of this place.

Hell, he still might.

"Good evening," Charlotte greeted, her gaze fixed on Billy. Out of habit, Ross rose from his seat, manners drilled into him from birth. Even as he stood, with his pal following suit, that soft, low voice slipped underneath Ross's suit jacket and his shirt, stroking over his skin. Even before they'd become lovers, that husky tone had reminded him of tangled sheets, throats sore and chafed from pleasure-soaked screams. "I'm Head Chef Charlotte Jarrett here at Sheen. I hope the meal is to your liking and you're enjoying your experience with us tonight." Then, just when Ross believed she wouldn't acknowledge him at all, she peered at him and dipped her chin. "Hello, Ross. It's good to see you again."

Lie.

The word scalded his tongue, roared in his head. She was as happy to see him sitting in her restaurant as he was to be here.

"You two know each other?" Billy asked as they lowered back into their chairs, saving Ross from having to reply to that fake smile and sentiment. His friend glanced back and forth between the two of them, a small frown creasing his brow even as curiosity lit his blue eyes.

"Yes," Ross ground out, then inhaled, deliberately releasing a breath and relaxing his clenched jaw. "Charlotte worked as the head chef at Elegance Ranch several years ago," he said, referring to the Edmond family ranch. Then added, "Before she moved to California for another job."

Damn, why had he added that? Yes, she'd moved; it was in the past, and he no longer gave a damn. But still… What the hell was she doing back in Royal?

"What a small world." Billy did the tennis match back-and-forth once more. "California?" His buddy arched a dark eyebrow. "What part, if you don't mind me asking?"

"Santa Monica," she replied evenly, still wearing that damn polite smile he detested. He recognized it; her mask, he'd called it. She'd always given it to his father, but never Ross.

Until now.

"I love Santa Monica. It's a wonderful city. Not that Royal isn't just as beautiful. But California's loss is our gain." Billy smiled warmly and rose once more, extending his hand toward Charlotte. "Well, since you and Ross don't need to introduce yourselves, allow me.

Billy Holmes, and it's a pleasure to meet such a lovely and talented chef."

"Thank you." Charlotte took his hand into hers, and even though it was just a simple press of palms, Ross had to fight back an inane urge to lurch to his feet and step in between them, to prevent his college friend—whom he trusted as much as his brother and sister—from touching her. But she'd revoked that privilege three years ago, and he didn't want to request it again. "Are you enjoying your meals?"

"Yes," Billy praised. "We had your braised beef signature dish, and it's delicious. I can't say I've tasted better."

"Thank you," she repeated, real warmth entering her smile. "Then I'd suggest trying our signature dessert, as well. A peach meringue torte with chocolate crumbles and a dollop of Chantilly cream."

"We'll take it. How can we say no to that?" Billy chuckled, reclaiming his seat. But clearly, he wasn't ready to let Charlotte go, much to Ross's aggravation.

Shit. How much longer did he have to sit here and pretend as if he couldn't catch her sweet yet sharp scent of sugar and figs. If he'd been blindfolded and set in a room full of people, he could still detect her delectable essence. Still locate *her*.

"I'll place your dessert order myself," she said. "Thank you both—" for only the second time since she arrived at their table, she quickly glanced at him, then away "—for joining us at Sheen tonight. If you'll excuse me—"

"Wait, Chef, one more moment of your time, please," Billy called out, and Ross narrowed his eyes on him. Jesus, what now? He needed Charlotte away from him before he did something stupid. Like escort her out of this restaurant and demand answers. Or commit the cardinal sin of digging his fingers underneath that neat bun at the back of her head and loosening it, freeing her dark brown hair to see if it still contained that same coarse silk texture. Discover if it still swept her shoulder blades or if she'd cut it. Find out whether she'd emit that same low gasp if he fisted the thick strands and tugged, whether her eyes would darken with desire...

Yeah, she had to go.

"Sure," Charlotte said, her tone even, and if Ross hadn't been studying her so closely, he would've missed the flicker of impatience in her eyes. That, too, he easily remembered about her. Cooking, *creating* had been her number one passion, and she had to be chafing at this dog and pony show when she could be back in her precious kitchen. "What can I do for you?"

"Well, we're—" Billy waved a hand toward Ross and then back at himself "—working on a luxury food, art and wine festival called Soiree on the Bay, to be held late July on Appaloosa Island. Are you familiar with it?"

"Yes." She nodded, her focus fully trained on Billy... and only the rapid beat of her pulse at the base of her neck betrayed her agitation. Right now, she probably wished the collar of her chef's jacket fully covered her neck. Because if it did, he wouldn't guess that she was most likely recalling the time he'd secretly taken her to the small, private island in Trinity Bay that his family owned. He'd escorted her there in her first helicopter ride, though it was also accessible by private ferry and airplane. They'd spent a lazy day and sizzling night at the boutique resort on the pristine beaches that occupied the western side of the island along with several large vacation homes.

Man, the things they'd done to each other in their room…

He shifted in his chair, unbidden lust burning an incendiary path through him at the sultry, hot memories of slick skin sliding against slick skin. Of groans punctuated by greedy whimpers and blissful laughter. Of moonlight streaming across sheets wrapped around tangled limbs.

Her gaze slid toward him, and for a long moment, their eyes clashed. Was she as steeped in the illicit past as he was? Did that sweet, tight flesh, which even now he could feel wrapped around his cock, pulse and dampen with liquid heat from those recollections? His own body throbbed so hard he feared one abrupt move could crack him down the middle.

He glanced away first.

"We're already in plans to develop the eastern side of the island," Billy said. "The festival is going to be huge, and we already have vendors lined up, with tickets projected to sell out within hours. Would you consider hosting a tent for the event? For Sheen?"

Ross jerked in surprise. The hell? They hadn't discussed this. He stared at his friend, but Billy continued aiming the full force of his charm on Charlotte. No. Just…no. Spend more time around his ex-lover? Have her involved in this event that could change the trajectory of his career. His *life*? He couldn't have a split focus; he couldn't afford it. And then… She didn't deserve to be involved in this project that meant so much to him. *She'd* walked away. *She'd* left him. So she didn't get to benefit from what was *his*.

And yes, he acknowledged how fucking petty that made him sound. But he didn't give a damn.

"I—" She frowned, shaking her head. "I'm flattered that you're asking, but I can't give you an answer without conferring with the owner and the management team."

"Please, do that and let us know your answer. With the thousands of people—both potential customers and clients—attending the festival, it could be advantageous for us and for Sheen. Not to mention you, personally, Chef. You're the magic behind the food, and as beautiful as the design and decor are and professional the service, it's the food that makes or breaks a restaurant. I believe this could be a huge opportunity for you."

Billy paused and tilted his head to the side. "In the meantime, while you're thinking the invitation over, would you also consider something else?" He chuckled, the sound self-deprecating. "I know we just met, and I'm already throwing a lot at you. But we're compiling an advisory board for the festival, and we're seeking the best creative minds in Texas. I've heard you're one of them, and it'd be an honor and asset to have you take part in it."

He'd heard she was creative—where? *When?* Ross had been under the impression that the other man hadn't known of Charlotte until five minutes before he'd asked to meet the chef after raving over their meal. Which, Ross grudgingly had to admit, had been exquisite. But then again, he expected nothing less from a woman who placed her career over everything else. She hadn't even cared that she'd left her parents behind.

Or me.

He locked that irritating and insidious thought down. Because that was in the past. His pride had been hurt. But as his reputation had proven, he was over it—over *her*.

Besides, he'd never give one woman that much sway over him again.

For the first time, unease crept across Charlotte's features, and he damn near felt the tension emanating off her. *Say no*, he silently ordered her.

"I don't—"

"Excuse me, I'm so sorry for interrupting." The server who'd escorted Charlotte to their table appeared, shooting an apologetic glance at Ross and Billy before addressing Charlotte. "Chef, your babysitter called. There's an emergency with Ben. He's running a fever, and she needs to know if she should take him to urgent care. Also—" her voice dropped but not low enough that Ross couldn't catch her next words "—she said he's crying for you."

Charlotte recoiled as if the words had been physical blows, her shoulders actually curling in before she jerked them back. Maybe remembering she had an audience. Because when she turned back to him and Billy, she'd carefully composed her features into a smooth mask.

If only he had the same superpower.

A baby? Charlotte had *a baby*? Shock, bone-deep, chilling and sickening, swam through him, burrowing to the dark soul that he'd believed too jaded to be stunned by anything.

"I'm sorry," she said in a calm tone that belied the worry gleaming in her coffee-colored eyes. Worry and... something else. And that something else had the hair on the nape of his neck prickling, standing at soldier-straight attention. If it had been anyone else, he'd have called that quicksilver emotion in her gaze fear. But he had to be mistaken. Sure, there wasn't any love lost between them, but why in the hell would she be afraid of him? His stomach twisted, clenched. "I need to go, but I'll place your dessert order. I hope the rest of your evening here at Sheen is—"

"You have a son?" he rasped, only the second time he'd spoken to her since she'd arrived at the table.

Again, that flash of something-that-couldn't-be-fear glinted in her eyes. And he wanted to erupt from his seat and demand she either stop looking at him like that or, better yet, explain why just glancing at him caused that reaction.

"Yes," she abruptly answered. Then, nodding, she edged back a step. "Again, thank you for dining with us."

With that, she whirled on her heel and quickly wound a path through the tables toward the rear of the restaurant. Ross stared after her retreating figure, frowning.

Don't even think about going after her. Keep your ass in this chair.

He growled that at his conscience, at the muscles in his thighs that already bunched in preparation of launching him from his seat. This restaurant—and her

son—were her business. Not his. She was no longer his
concern and hadn't been for three years.

"Did I overstep there?" Billy murmured, picking up
his fork and flipping it between his fingers. It had been
a nervous gesture of his since college—a small tell in
an otherwise confident and self-possessed demeanor.
"I should've checked with you first to ensure you were
okay with me asking her to be a vendor and a member
of the advisory board."

"It's fine," Ross said, waving off his friend's concern.

It wasn't, though. But damn if he would explain to
Billy why.

No one knew of his and Charlotte's affair from years
ago. They'd kept it secret for the obvious reason—him
having sex with his employee had been inappropriate,
at best. At worst, it was a power imbalance that he'd
been too entitled, too damn infatuated and desperate
for her to acknowledge. He'd justified it by convincing
himself he'd never be the kind of asshole that would
fire her if—no, *when*—their affair ended.

His father was that kind of asshole, though. His son
involved with a staff member? Hell no. Rusty Edmond
possessed enough good ol' boy in him to rate that sin
just under murder but above stealing.

That had been cause enough to keep their…relation-
ship quiet. But he'd harbored another, more private one.

Charlotte had been his. His choice. His beauty. His
secret haven from a world where he was judged by his
name, his reputation. His entire life, his father had determined his schools, career, even the women he'd
dated. But Charlotte? She'd been the one person—the
one decision—that had been strictly his own.

She'd been special.

But he couldn't tell Billy that—couldn't tell anyone. And even if he'd been free to, he still wouldn't. Because in some ways, Charlotte still remained the only autonomous decision in his life. And despite everything, he treasured that.

"Are you sure? I—" Billy frowned, his lips snapping closed as he studied Ross.

"What?" he asked, just shy of a snap. He wanted to be done with this conversation, hell, this restaurant that seemed to bear the stamp of Charlotte in its walls, in the decor, even in the scent of its food. Now that he knew she was the chef here—that she was back in Royal— she permeated everything.

"Fine. I'm just going to say it," Billy said, setting the fork down and leaning back in his chair. "I might be out of line here, but there seemed to be…tension between you two. Am I wrong?"

"Yes," Ross clipped out, but then inhaled, forcibly relaxing his jaw. "Yes," he repeated, this time more evenly. "Charlotte was our head chef for a while before she left for another job opportunity. We were amicable, but that's it. Nothing more, nothing less."

"Okay, if you say so. I believe you." But that steady, unwavering stare didn't shift from Ross's face, and he smothered the urge to snap at his friend again. Finally, Billy shrugged a shoulder and picked up his wine. "She's a beautiful woman," he observed before sipping from his glass. "And obviously talented and successful. So you wouldn't have a problem with me asking her out? There wouldn't be an issue because she used to be your employee?"

"Of course not," Ross growled. Yes, honest-to-God *growled*. Because just the thought of Billy's fingers spanning that slender waist or cupping that dramatic flare of hips had him clenching his own wineglass so hard he feared it might shatter under the pressure. "I don't have any claim on her. She was just our chef, for God's sake. Do what you want."

The words, the tone sounded angry to his own ears, so when the other man said nothing but pinned him with a speculative look, Ross didn't challenge him on it. Didn't snarl out another protest. Why bother? He didn't believe his own damn self.

"I'm just going to say this, then leave it alone," Billy murmured. "From one friend to another, whatever is eating at you? Deal with it before it deals with you. Now—" he took another sip of wine and set his glass on the table "—as for the advisory board, I was also thinking about approaching Lila Jones from the Royal Chamber of Commerce…"

Ross went along with the subject change, nodding and replying when appropriate. But his mind had drifted back to the past. To that day when she'd ended their affair. When she'd announced that she was moving to California. He'd been angry. Hurtful. Harsh. Not because he'd been in love—he hadn't believed in that emotion then any more than he did today. Yet, it had shown him that wanting something for himself—believing someone could want him just for him—was a dream better left behind for the boy who'd once believed in superheroes, purple, singing dinosaurs and mothers who stayed.

And he'd stopped dreaming long ago.

Three

There were worse things in life than listening to your mother complain and nag. For instance, volcanoes exploding and drowning whole cities under their molten flow of lava. Wars that left countries devastated and torn. Pandemic viruses infecting the population and turning them into hordes of flesh-eating zombies.

Firefly being canceled.

Yes, so many worse things than having to sit quietly while your mother criticized your parenting.

But right now, Charlotte wouldn't mind a zombie bursting into her house and chasing her around her kitchen. It would definitely be a good excuse to end this phone call.

Smothering a sigh, she pinched the bridge of her nose and prayed for patience. "Mom, I'm sorry I didn't tell you myself about Ben, and that you had to hear about it when you called the restaurant," she apologized. *Again.* "As soon as I got home, I rushed him to the emergency room. But I promise I would've called you this morning."

"It was just so humiliating and hurtful to find out from an employee, instead of my daughter, that my grandson was sick," Cherise Jarrett harped. Only the genuine hurt in her mother's voice kept Charlotte from snapping back in irritation. "I know we've…had our differences in the past few years, Charlotte, but we love Ben, and when we couldn't reach you…"

Had our differences. What a nice way of saying "estranged because you got knocked up and had a kid out of wedlock."

But she clenched her teeth, locking the sarcastic words down. Wasn't this part of the reason she'd returned to Royal? To try to heal the fractured relationship between her and her parents? She'd disappointed them three years ago when she'd called with the news that she was pregnant, but they'd also disappointed her with their reaction.

Brian and Cherise Jarrett had always been strict, conservative but loving parents. Charlotte had expected them to be worried and upset by her news, but not to practically disown her. Nor for them to be relieved that she moved to California so they could avoid gossip about their daughter having an illegitimate child. If not for her sister, brother-in-law and niece in California, Charlotte would've been all alone in the world. Her parents' rejection and disapproval had been like a dagger to the chest, and for months she'd felt adrift, no longer anchored by their love and friendship.

But Charlotte had to give her parents credit. Once Ben was born, their cold demeanor had thawed. Her son and their love for him had helped bridge the divide that had sprung up between them seven months prior. Even if they allowed people to assume that she'd married and divorced while in California, and Ben was the child of that union. Yeah, that continued to sting. Still, now that she'd moved back to Royal with Ben so they could be closer to her parents, she hoped that distance, and the hurt, would disappear altogether.

Then there were days like today…

"They made me shut off my cell phone at the hospital, and it was after 2:00 a.m. when we arrived home. I didn't want to wake you and Dad. Especially when Ben was fine. If it'd been more serious, I would've found a way to contact you guys. But his fever broke while we were there, and the doctor said it's likely nothing more than a twenty-four-hour bug. So please don't worry."

"Still—"

"What was so important you had to call me at the restaurant?" Charlotte interrupted, hopefully diverting the subject. She had to try before she opened the cabinet where she hid the emergency bourbon and poured it into her coffee.

"Well, it doesn't seem such an emergency now, but…" Her mom paused, and Charlotte's stomach clamped down tight on the unease twisting through her. Silly to feel this way. And at one time in their relationship, she wouldn't have. Instead, she would've teased her mother about being dramatic. But that wasn't their relationship anymore. Now Charlotte tensed, unsure what to expect, bracing herself against what was possibly to come. "But the caterer for the church's Women's Day celebration backed out at the last minute. The event is in two weeks, and I wanted to see if you could step in with small appetizers and finger foods. Nothing too fancy, since I know this is short notice..."

"Sure, Mom," Charlotte murmured, even as *Are you out of your mind?* rang in her head. She already had so much on her plate, yet she didn't rescind her agreement. Her parents had always supported her dream of being a chef even though they'd envisioned her following in the footsteps of her father and sister as an attorney.

And when was the last time her mother had asked anything from her?

No, that part of her that still longed to please her parents, and hungered for their smiles of approval and love, couldn't turn her mom down. "Send me a list of the food you were thinking of, the place and time of the event, and when you need me there to set up."

"Thank you, Charlotte," her mother breathed, relief flooding through their connection. "You have no idea how much I appreciate your help and jumping in at the last minute."

"You're welcome." And for the first time since she answered the phone, she smiled, a warm glow pulsing in her chest. "I'll get—" She broke off as the doorbell echoed through the house. "I'm sorry, Mom, that's the door. I need to go. But I'll check back in with you later about Ben. Don't forget to send me the information."

"I won't. And give that beautiful boy a huge hug and kiss from his grandma."

"I will," she promised. "Talk to you later."

Ending the call, Charlotte strode from the kitchen down the short hall toward the front door. She glanced down at her smartwatch, noting the time with a frown. Nine twenty. Who would show up at her house so early on a Friday morning? Even Faith didn't call her until after twelve because Charlotte had made it known that her mornings belonged to Ben. And she'd already called and left a message with both Faith and Jeremy Randall, the owner, to inform them she wouldn't be in today because her son was still under the weather.

Her thoughts drifted to Ben as she pushed aside the curtain over the window bracketing the front door. He had still been napping when her mother called, but she needed to check on him—

Jesus.

Her arm dropped like a leaden weight to her side, the curtain drifting back into place as she helplessly stared at the window.

No. It couldn't be. God wasn't that unkind.

But she doubted God had anything to do with who stood on her porch. All that credit belonged to the guy a lot farther south.

She squeezed her eyes shut, and as if of its own volition, her hand rose to her neck, fingers lightly stroking the necklace underneath her long-sleeved shirt. As soon as she realized what her wayward fingers were doing, she jerked her arm back down. *Dammit.* As much as she fervently wished otherwise, nothing could change the fact that he stood on the other side of her door.

The thunderous pounding of her heart and the rush of her pulse in her head only validated it.

She could pretend not to be home. Avoid him. After all, he'd shown up at her house unannounced and definitely uninvited. This wasn't Sheen, and she didn't have to speak to him. Or look at him. Drown in those eyes that both threatened frostbite and to consign her to flames. Inhale his masculine, earthy, *raw* scent that carried notes of sandalwood, man and sex. Burn in the contempt that leaped from him in rolling waves of heat.

She owed it to herself, and especially to Ben, to protect her son at all costs. Because the alternative was… unthinkable.

Fear fissured through her, its impact stealing her breath. Ross believed she'd "gotten rid of him," as he and Rusty had ordered her to, three years ago. What would he do if he found out she hadn't obeyed his command…

The doorbell pealed again.

Dammit. Her fingers curled into her palms, the short fingernails digging into her flesh.

She wasn't a coward. Ross Edmond no longer wielded any power over her. He was a nonfactor, and to not answer that door and hide would mean he affected her emotions, her life. And she refused to grant that to him.

Before she could talk herself out of it, she twisted the lock and doorknob, flinging the door open.

Maybe she should've taken a few extra minutes…

Yes, she'd just seen Ross last night, but those hours hadn't inoculated her against the force of his presence. Three years and over a thousand miles' distance should've been enough. But that had been wishful thinking on her part.

Silently, she shuffled backward, and his ice-blue

gaze didn't shift from her face as he stepped inside her home. Which was fair, she supposed, since she couldn't remove hers from his.

It wasn't fair.

Someone who led the dissolute lifestyle of a playboy should wear the corruption of it on his skin, his body. Like a masochist, she'd occasionally done a Google search of Ross's name over the years. And every time, an image of him with a different woman as they emerged from this party or that club had popped into the feed.

But no. His golden skin remained as unblemished and smooth as ever. His lean, broad-shouldered body stood as straight and powerful as before. The wide, carnal curves of his mouth still promised sex and sin. Those penetrating, bright blue eyes were as clear and incisive as she remembered.

Not that she could ever forget the arrogant slashes of his cheekbones or the patrician slope of his nose or the strong, bold facial structure. Every day she looked into her son's features, she saw Ross. Was reminded of the man who'd fathered her beautiful little boy and rejected them both.

She couldn't escape him.

Couldn't forgive him.

The reminder of his unpardonable offense—not wanting her or the baby they'd created together— wrenched her from the dazzling tapestry he'd always been capable of weaving around her. He might have the appearance of an archangel, but he possessed the morals and heart of one of the fallen brethren.

"Ross," she greeted flatly, closing the door with a

soft, definitive click. "This is a surprise." *What are you doing here? How did you know where I lived? When are you leaving?* She slid a surreptitious glance down the hall toward Ben's room. He needed to go before her son woke from his nap. "What can I do for you?"

He didn't immediately answer but surveyed the postage-stamp-sized foyer with its generic paintings and cherry wood mantel that had come with the home. The living room opened up off to the left, with the large bay windows, small gas fireplace, overstuffed couch and love seat, and the glass coffee table visible. From his vantage point, he couldn't glimpse the connecting dining room with its long, cedar table and chairs that seated eight people, or the pretty chandelier that hung from the tall ceiling.

Her home couldn't compare to the palatial Elegance Ranch where his family lived and where she'd once ruled the dream of a kitchen that could compete with any restaurant's commercial space. But this single-level, two-bedroom, two-bath house was comfortable, cozy and more than enough for her and Ben.

"You have a nice place," he finally said, his glacial gaze resting on her once more.

"Thank you," she replied, refusing to shiver under that stare. "That's not why you're here, though, is it?"

A corner of his mouth lifted in a just-short-of-humorous half smile. "Still direct, I see," he murmured.

No, she'd never been that direct with him. Not that honest, either.

If she had been honest—if she'd trusted him enough to be—she would've confessed how she hadn't felt safe at Elegance Ranch in those last couple of months she worked there. How his father had been steadily hitting on her. Rusty Edmond hadn't touched her, but the flirting, the sly compliments and innuendos…those, in a way, had been more insidious. Because if she confided in others, they could wave it off as harmless, warning her she didn't have concrete evidence to complain. And complain to whom? Her boss? The very man who made her feel uncomfortable and threatened?

Threatened, because if she dared called Rusty on his actions, he would've fired her. And he probably wouldn't have just stopped here. With his power and privilege, he could've destroyed her career as easily as he ordered a rare T-bone steak for dinner. She'd felt trapped, cornered. Defenseless. And the only way out that she'd seen was leaving.

She'd could've told Ross about the situation with his father; she'd been tempted to confess all. But every time she gathered the courage, something held her back. No, not something. *Fear*.

Fear that he wouldn't believe her.

Fear that he would believe her and still side with his father over her.

He was an Edmond first. And his family took precedence over everything—and everyone.

"I have things to take care of before I leave for the restaurant, so…" She trailed off, letting her not-so-subtle hint to get on with it linger in the air between them. The most important subject she hadn't been direct or honest with him about lay sleeping down the hall. She needed Ross out of the house. Five minutes ago.

He nodded, sliding his hands into the front pockets of his pants, the motion opening his suit jacket. And she tried to convince herself that she didn't remember how wide and strong his chest had been. How that divot in the middle of his pecs had been perfect for resting her cheek. How hard and muscled that delicious ladder of abs had been between her thighs when she straddled him.

Tried and failed.

"Two reasons. First, I wanted to check on your baby. How is he feeling this morning?" he murmured.

"He's fine. Better," she amended, hesitant.

Why would he care? No hint of anger threaded through his voice... Oh, God, wait. He'd said *baby*. How old did he think Ben was? Did he assume she'd had a child with another man? Relief trickled through her. But underneath, winding through like a silver thread, lurked an irrational fury. He hadn't wanted their baby, so how dare he show concern over another man's.

Fucking great. Now she was getting all fired up over an imaginary partner who'd supposedly fathered her child.

This was what being around Ross Edmond for five minutes did to her.

"The father," he hedged, his voice slightly deepening even as his words confirmed her suspicion. "Where is he?" Once more he scanned her home. "Did he move back with you?"

She barely smothered her snort. "His father isn't in the picture." Not a lie. "It's just us," she added, skirting him and heading into the living room.

Not because she relished the idea of him having more access to her house, her private sanctuary. She would be a fool not to guard her life, her secret against him.

But she also needed to be free of that tiny space where his scent filled her nostrils, sat on her tongue, clung to her clothes, her skin. She just craved a breath that didn't carry *him*.

Ross stared at her, his crystalline gaze unreadable before he glanced away, a muscle ticking along his jaw. "Charlotte, I—" he ground out, thrusting a hand through the longer strands of dirty blond hair that waved away from his face.

"What else, Ross?" she interrupted him, not bothering to prevent the edge from creeping into her voice. She tried not to glance down at her watch, but the minutes steadily ticking by before Ben woke drummed against her skin like impatient fingertips. "You said there were two reasons you stopped by."

For a moment he studied her, flint in his eyes and the sculpted length of his jaw still tight. "Last night, Billy asked you about joining the advisory board for the festival. It was awkward as hell for him to put you on the spot like that, and I understand if you decide against it. But I wanted to see if you'd made a decision."

"You couldn't have called and asked me this?"

"I don't have your number."

"No," she shot back. "But somehow you found out where I lived, so unearthing my phone number probably wouldn't have been that much of a leap."

"Touché," he murmured, his lips quirking in that maddening—and damn sexy—half smile that had never failed to tempt her into stroking her fingers across his mouth. Three years ago, she could, and did, submit to that urge. Now she curled her fingers into her palms, convincing herself that the itch tingling in her fingertips and palms had zero to do with that old impulse. "You've been away from Royal three years, but surely you haven't forgotten how not much remains secret around here. It didn't take but asking the right question of the right person to find out where you'd moved to. Just making that clear so you don't think I took up a second career as a stalker in your absence."

She snorted, crossing her arms over her chest. He spoke the truth. And she hadn't missed the "everybody knows your name and your business" mentality of this small Texas town.

Of course, she and Ross had achieved the miraculous. Their affair had been one of the best-kept secrets in Royal.

Until she'd outed them to Rusty, that is.

"Right. About that." She shook her head, loosening her arms to hold her palms up. "I'm sure your friend meant well, but given our…past, it's probably not a good idea for me to be on your advisory board."

"Last night, I agreed with you. But I've been thinking…" His gaze narrowed on her, and she resisted falling into that storm of ice and heat.

"Thinking what?" she prodded.

"That the success of this festival, Soiree on the Bay, is important to a lot of people. With that in mind, I'm willing to put aside our *past*—" his lips twisted as he mimicked her word "—to achieve that goal. And this advisory board is part of that. We need the best creative and forward-thinking minds in this group. And whatever happened between us, I remember you were a brilliant, innovative chef. You can bring that originality, imagination as well as your business sense to the board. It can only benefit all of us."

What had that silent but deafening pause been about? What was he *not* saying? She gave her head a hard, mental shake. None of her business. She couldn't afford to get bogged down in anything Ross. In anything Edmond.

Been there, done that. Had the stretch marks to prove it.

"I'll consider what you're saying, Ross." She absolutely would *not*. "But I can't make any pro—"

"Mama."

A light patter of rapid footsteps followed the plaintive, soft and utterly sweet voice calling out to her. Chubby arms wrapped around her lower calf, and in spite of the dread pumping through her veins like a freight train and flooding her mouth with the metallic taste of fear, she knelt to the floor and pulled her son into her arms. His arms wound around her neck, and he burrowed close. Her heart hammered against her ribs, threatening to break each of them, but she still placed a gentle kiss on top of Ben's thick, light brown curls, breathing in his precious scent. She squeezed her eyes against the sting of tears that suddenly pricked her eyes. Not just because one day he would lose that sweet baby smell.

The abrupt rush of overwhelming sadness and dismay was due to the silent man who loomed several feet away from them. The man whose gaze seared her like a flaming hot brand.

The Sword of Damocles that had hung over her life— over Ben's life—had suddenly fallen.

And there was nothing she could do to sweep them out from under its crashing, lethal weight.

"How're you feeling, baby boy?" she asked, pressing the back of her hand to his forehead and then to his cheek. Relief was a soothing balm inside her at the coolness of his skin. No fever. Thank God. No mother ever felt as helpless as when her child was sick.

"Good," he mumbled, crowding closer to her, his arms tightening as he notched his head under her chin and tried to crawl up her torso. In spite of the bile churning in her belly and burning an acidic path toward her throat, she smiled. Ben was a friendly, bubbly child with seemingly endless energy—except when he fell ill. Then he clung to her, not wanting to let her out of his sight. Not that she minded. Holding him, having his small, sturdy body pressed close, and listening to him breathe were just small things to reassure her that her baby was okay. "Eat," he demanded. "Hungry." Even though the order sounded more like "hungwy," she fully understood it.

"You want banana pancakes?" she asked, suggesting his favorite breakfast. Okay, so sue her. She was spoiling him this morning.

He nodded, his tawny curls brushing her chin. "'Nana 'cakes. Juice."

"You got it." She pressed another kiss to the top of his head. "Can you go play with your trucks for a minute while I finish talking to this nice man?" She fought to maintain her soft, even tone, but with her heart lodged in her throat, it was becoming more of a struggle.

For the first time, Ben turned his head and looked at Ross. Shy with strangers, he didn't say anything, but the panic crackling inside her, dancing over her skin like a live wire, ratcheted to a higher, dissonant level. Her son stared at his father for the first time, although he didn't know it. It was a surreal moment. Father and son studying one another... Especially Ross, with that narrowed, enigmatic scrutiny...

Part of her wanted to thrust Ben behind her, shield him from Ross. Protect him and yell that she wouldn't allow him to hurt her son.

But the other half... That proud, almost smug half yearned to stand Ben before him, let Ross get a good, long look and brag that this was the precious, brilliant and perfect boy that he'd wanted her to get rid of. That he'd wanted nothing to do with.

That vindictive, ugly part of her wanted him to soak, fucking *drown* in regret.

Did that make her a bitch? Probably. Still, the primal need to protect Ben superseded any petty desires.

"You play for a few, then we'll eat banana pancakes." She stood and, taking his tiny hand in hers, led him to the corner of the living room with a trunk full of his toys. After removing a couple of trucks and making sure he was entertained, she inhaled a deep breath that did absolutely nothing for her nerves and turned to face Ross. Jerking her head toward the foyer, she said, "Over here."

She didn't wait for him to agree but strode out of the living room and returned to the small entryway. There would be questions; one glance in his glacial gaze and she could practically see the suspicion crowded there. But she wouldn't have this conversation within earshot of her son.

"I thought he was a baby," Ross murmured, but she didn't mistake that low tone for calm. Not when she noted the thunder rumbling underneath. "And you let me think that."

She didn't wilt under the dark accusation in his voice. Didn't flinch from it. It wasn't *her* fault that he'd assumed she had an infant instead of a toddler.

Ross shifted his stare away from her and back to the living room. Silence descended between them, and in the cramped foyer, the weight of it threatened to crush her. Again, she fought the urge to jump in between them, guard her son from that razor-sharp speculation, that ice-cold face. She silently ordered her arms to remain by her sides instead of wrapping around her torso in a telltale, too vulnerable gesture of self-preservation.

"How old is he?" he snapped, the frost melting under the steam of the heat throbbing in that deep, raw timbre.

"Ben is two," she replied, reaching for and clinging to a calm that was as fake as the flowers in the vase behind her.

"Two," Ross rasped, still not removing his eyes from the little boy who crashed trucks together, complete with sound effects. Blissfully ignorant to the jarring tension that hissed and popped just feet away from him. "The eyes," he continued in that same hoarse voice that almost hurt her ears. "They're you. The hair, the skin, they're…" *They're both of us*, she silently finished for him. Skin just a shade darker than his light brown curls—curls that were softer than hers but a little coarser than Ross's hair. Ben was a beautiful melding of his genetics and hers. "But his face, his features… It's like looking at a picture of me as a kid."

She still didn't say anything as he sussed out who Ben was to him. Instead, she stood silent as he swung his attention back to her, stoically witnessing the succession of emotions that marched through his expression. Shock. Disbelief. Rage. And something not as simple, but just as dark and powerful. But then the rage returned, capsizing everything else until lightning flashed in the sky blue of his eyes. The fury tautened the skin over his cheekbones, his jaw, until the bones seemed ready to slice through. His sensual mouth flattened, tightened until only a cruel slant remained.

"Is he my son?" he growled. "And think carefully before you answer me, Charlotte. Especially since the evidence is staring me in the face. Don't lie to me."

"Why would I need to lie to you?" She notched up her chin, defiant, but unable to quell the shiver jetting down her spine, vibrating through her. "Ben is yours."

If possible, his eyes brightened, so hot with fury that her skin bore the brunt of that heat.

"You didn't think I had a right to know? If I hadn't shown up here today, would you even have deigned to inform me that the son *I didn't know existed* lived in the same goddamn town as me?"

"Lower your voice and watch your mouth," she snapped, and even though every self-protective instinct in her roared a warning to keep her distance, she shifted closer to avoid even the chance of Ben overhearing them. "And the answer is no, I wouldn't have told you. Don't try to turn this around on me," she hissed, her own hurt and anger burning through the coolness of her tone to leave it trembling. God, she hated that it trembled. She hated any sign of weakness in front of this man. The last time she'd betrayed her vulnerability with him, he'd shut her down. *Rejected* her. He would never get the chance again. "You decided you didn't want him, didn't want to upset your life with the inconvenience of a baby. So I don't owe you a damn thing, nor do we need anything from you. I made the decision to become both mother and father to him, so you don't get to act the victim now."

"What the hell are you talking about? You never—" He shook his head, his hand slashing between them. "Not here. And not now. I don't give a fuck what you believe your reasons were to lie and keep my son away from me. Just so it's clear, there *isn't* a good enough reason," he snarled.

"To protect my son from being hurt is a damn excellent reason. The best," she hurled back.

"Protect him from his father?" A quicksilver emotion flashed in his eyes, and if she'd believed Ross capable of feeling anything beyond lust, pride and self-gratification, she might've called it pain. His face hardened further, and he shifted backward. As if being in such close contact with her disgusted him.

Screw. Him.

And screw herself for that thin sliver of pain that slid between her ribs and buried right in her heart.

"I want a DNA test done."

She tilted her head to the side, arching an eyebrow. "I thought he was the image of you as a child. Now you're questioning his paternity. That turnaround was quick," she drawled, offended that he would dare doubt Ben.

Dare doubt me.

The shifty, taunting whisper brushed across her mind

before she could smother it. No, she didn't care if he doubted her. She didn't care how he thought about her at all, because he didn't matter.

Only Ben did.

His lip curled into a derisive sneer. "I don't question whether he's mine. It's you and your motives that I have zero trust in. So before I can make my next move, I need concrete, *legal* proof that he's mine so you can't deny me access to him."

Her breath stalled in her throat, and she stumbled back. On a low curse, Ross moved, reaching for her, but she batted away his hands, forcing her knees to strengthen, willing every ounce of the meager strength she retained to her legs.

Though so much fear poured through her that she ached with it, she managed to speak the dreaded words. "What is that supposed to mean?" she pressed. "Before you make your next move?"

His gaze crystallized, and his big, lean body straightened so he seemed to loom larger. More intimidating. "I'll be in touch, Charlotte. Word of advice—don't even consider pulling another vanishing act like you did three years ago. This time I will follow."

With those ominous words echoing in the foyer and ringing in her ears, he crossed the short space to the door, jerked it open and exited through it.

She didn't move—couldn't, even though Ben waited on her. Ross's statement rooted her to the floor.

His next move.

What was he planning? Custody? Taking Ben from her? With the full weight of the Edmond name and the power of their money and connections behind him, he could. He might—

No.

The objection slammed into her head, and she fisted her fingers. No, she wouldn't allow him to rip her baby from her arms. Not when Ross had been the first one to walk away, to abandon them both.

She shoved away from the wall, resolve gelling inside her, fortifying her.

She was no longer that lonely, needy girl who'd left Royal and nearly begged him not to turn his back on her and their baby. Motherhood had made her a warrior.

If Ross wanted a battle, then a battle was what he would get.

Four

He had a son.

Ross stared at the paternity report that had been emailed to him a couple of hours earlier. For what could've been the hundredth time, he scanned it, his gaze settling on the line at the bottom that changed his life forever.

"The alleged father is not excluded as the biological father of the tested child. The probability of paternity is 99.9998 percent."

His pulse roared in his head, the thunderous crash of sound a sonorous backdrop for the seething cauldron of emotion boiling over in his chest. Shock. Fear. Pain. Joy.

God, so much joy.

Until the moment three days ago when he'd stared down into a tiny face that could've been a replica of his twenty-five years ago... Until he'd met familiar brown eyes brimming with curiosity and shyness... Until then, children had been a "someday" notion that bore no place in his hedonistic life. But the moment Ross met his son, someday had become now, in an instant.

He'd wanted those brown eyes to reflect delight and love when they looked at him. Wanted those arms to lift to him in a show of faith and confidence.

Ross just longed to call that beautiful boy son. To claim him as his own. And to be claimed as father in return.

The intensity of that need burned so fiercely that his skin and bones almost couldn't contain the strength and power of that yearning.

His gaze scanned the report once more, passing over the name at the top. Benjamin Jarrett. *Ben.*

For some reason, he hadn't been able to say his son's name aloud at Charlotte's home. As if it were some kind of talisman that would make this too real. Real, only to be stolen from him with greedy, vicious hands.

But not now. Not with these paternity test results.

"Ben," he whispered, finally giving his newest but deepest hope voice, a name.

Even as a now recognizable and intimate anger stirred within him like a flickering, dancing flame. He'd been denied the first two years of his son's life, and Charlotte had denied their son his last name. She hadn't even given Ben that—given Ross that.

Did she really hate him that much? His fingers curled into a fist on top of his desk, the skin over his knuckles blanching before he deliberately relaxed his hand, extending each finger one by one. He inhaled, held the air in his lungs, then slowly released it, attempting to blow a cooling breath over his rage.

It didn't matter if she hated him or not. Or what her trumped-up reasons were. *She* had chosen to leave Royal. *She* had chosen not to tell him she was pregnant. *She* had chosen to rob him of his son. Every step of the way, Charlotte had made the decisions for all three of them, uncaring of the repercussions. Ben deserved both of them—a mother *and* a father.

And Ross was through letting her have all the power in their lives.

His desk phone intercom buzzed, interrupting his thoughts. "Ross." His assistant's voice echoed through the console speaker. "There's a Charlotte Jarrett here to see you."

Pressing the button, he ordered, "Send her in, please."

Rising from his office chair, he rounded the desk. Grim satisfaction thrummed within him. As soon as he received the paternity report, he'd texted Charlotte and asked her to come by his office so they could speak.

Those dots had bubbled for a while before she actually replied. But she'd agreed, and now that she stood on the other side of his office door, the anticipation of getting answers, of demanding his rights as a father to their baby coiled inside him like an agitated rattlesnake ready to strike.

The knock came a second before the door opened, revealing his assistant and Charlotte. But all he saw was *her*. It was that goddamn superpower of hers, that ability to dominate a man's attention so all else faded to blurred nothingness. Today she wore a short black leather jacket in deference to the February morning. A simple but formfitting white shirt emphasized the full curves of her breasts, and dark blue skinny jeans clung to her sensual, rounded hips and thick thighs. Camel-colored ankle boots elongated legs that already seemed to stretch for eternity.

She might as well have been wearing a couture ball gown with miles of skin revealed by strategic cutouts. Or nothing at all. She commanded every bit of his full, undivided attention. And even unwillingly, he complied.

With her, he'd never been able to do anything but be attuned to her.

To *want* her.

She'd left him, lied to him, kept his son from him. And yet, his dick didn't give a damn.

Yeah, if only it were that simple.

His cock had gotten hard for plenty of women over the years. But none had elicited this visceral, nearly primal hunger like Charlotte Jarrett had from the very first time he'd seen her in his father's study when Rusty had hired her.

If he could, he'd claw that traitorous part of him out of his body, his soul, wherever it hid inside him.

He tore his gaze away from Charlotte to nod at his assistant. "Thank you, Sandra. No interruptions for the next hour, please."

She nodded and left the office, closing the door behind her.

"Do you want to put your things down?" He gestured toward the large purse slung over her shoulder that was more akin to a messenger bag. "Can I take your coat?"

"No, thanks. I have to be at the restaurant soon, so can we get this over with?" she asked. The belligerent words belied the calm tone. The same calm tone she'd employed at her home before her temper had flared and she'd lit into him. "I assume you received the DNA results."

"I did," he said and waved a hand toward the couch and chairs in the sitting area. "Please sit."

"Really, Ross." Her lips twisted into what could've been called—incorrectly—a smile. "Pleasantries? We're past that, aren't we?" She shook her head and crossed her arms over her chest. Then, as if thinking better of the gesture, slowly lowered her arms to her sides. "I'd rather stand. And get to the point of this."

"The *point*, Charlotte? Okay, we'll do this your way. For the last time," he murmured, moving toward her.

He halted when several inches separated them. Far enough away that he couldn't accidentally touch her, but close enough that he could read the flash of apprehension in her eyes.

Did it make him an asshole that a dark gratification filled him at the sight of it?

Probably.

Fuck it. He owned it.

"The report confirmed that I'm Ben's father," he said, uttering those words aloud for the first time. Absorbing that punch of joy, shock and fear again.

"So now you know for certain." She notched her chin up, and in spite of the anger swirling through him like combustible fuel, he had to battle the need to grip that stubborn chin and cup the vulnerable nape of her neck and drag her closer. Had to smother the urge to slam his mouth to hers until she melted under him, until her lips parted for him…until all those soft, dangerous curves pressed to his frame, surrendering. He wanted to fuck the insolence out of her. Clenching his jaw, he resisted the lust, the grinding lure to conquer, to dominate. "What now?" she continued. "Because we both also know you have no interest in being a father—you didn't three years ago, and you didn't right up until you found out about Ben."

"You have no idea what I want. You've never *asked* me what I want," he snapped, bitterness coating his voice. "Every decision has been yours without thought or care to the consequences or who you were hurting."

"Because I've had to," she shouted back at him, the words bouncing off the walls, echoing in the room. A breath shuddered out from between her lips and, visibly shaken, she swept a hand over her thick brown hair. Straightening her shoulders, she sucked in a breath and glanced away from him.

Several seconds passed before she faced him again, and a mask had dropped over her features. Composed, she said, "You can't revise history to suit your narration, Ross. I did what I had to in order to care for my son. I've provided for him, and I'll continue to do so. I don't need or want your money, but this isn't about me. Child support is about Ben. So if you want to contribute, I'll set up an account for him, and the money can go toward his college education or whatever he decides to do with it when he's of age."

"How magnanimous of you to allow me to provide for *our* son," Ross drawled. "I hate to break it to you, Charlotte, but you can't keep me out of his life any longer. And if you would for just a second put your love for him ahead of your hate for me, you would see that he needs me, *his father*, in his."

"How fucking dare you?" she whispered, her eyes narrowing, but it was the telltale glistening in those brown depths that relayed the level of her anger. Charlotte only cried when her rage reached a level that it was either explode or crumble.

And Charlotte Jarrett never crumbled. She might cut bait and run, but collapse?

Not possible.

"All I've ever done from the moment I found out I was pregnant with Ben was put him first. I almost lost my relationship with my parents. I left my old life. I started over in a new city. I worked long hours. I put my goals on the back burner. *For. Him.* Always for him. And I don't regret a single one of those choices. So, hell no. You don't get to sit in judgment of me with your righteous indignation. Where were you, Ross? Playing the international playboy hopping from party to party, woman to woman, while I sacrificed and cared for Ben. *Loved* him."

"You didn't give me that choice, Charlotte. Didn't even grant me the damn option of deciding if I wanted to put aside that lifestyle and be in his life. So now you don't get to be a martyr and cast me in the role of devil because you made decisions all on your own without anyone else's input," he snarled.

"Please." She slashed a hand through the air. "You believe donating your DNA grants you some rights to him? You're wrong. An absentee father is better than one who will play with him like a shiny new toy, then abandon him as soon as something important like a social event, gala or business prospect pops up. Or better yet, a father who didn't want him in the first place."

"What the hell are you talking about...that I didn't want him in the first place?" he growled, latching on to the last accusation because trying to unpack the others lanced him to the core. Was that how she really saw him? A self-indulgent player who didn't give a damn about anything but the next good time and his dick? Was that the real reason she'd kept Ben from him? The pain bloomed in his chest, radiating outward in a toxic, blazing red mushroom. "You said that before, and I call bullshit. Because it implies that you gave me a choice. When you didn't, Charlotte. You stole two years of my son's life from me that I can never get back," he finished, voice hoarse with fury, hurt...grief.

He'd missed his son's first smile. His first word. His first step. Ross knew nothing about Ben. Not his favorite food or toy. Not how cranky he could be when he was tired. Not his laugh.

The hole that yawned wide inside him spread big enough for him to plummet into and never hit the bottom.

"Are you serious, Ross?" She speared him with a look of such disgust it rolled over his skin, polluting him. "Is this the game you're going to play? You don't remember telling me to get rid of our son?" She snorted. "Plausible deniability doesn't become you. Neither does playing dumb."

He almost lashed out with a reply designed to strike and hurt. But then her words penetrated his skull. *You don't remember telling me to get rid of our son?* The question ricocheted inside his head, and he almost stumbled back from the vileness of it. The acidic horror that crowded into his throat and spilled onto his tongue.

"Charlotte, please," he rasped. When she parted her lips, no doubt to blast him with more contempt, he held up a hand, palm out. "Just…pretend I don't know, and tell me. What do you mean I told you to get rid of Ben?"

She glared at him, her chest rising and falling on loud, staccato bursts of breath. For a moment he didn't believe she would grant him that. But then she shook her head, huffing out a hard chuckle. "This is crazy," she muttered but then waved a hand. "Fine. Where should I start this trip down memory lane?"

"The beginning. And leave nothing out."

"Right." Another abbreviated laugh that wasn't a laugh, and she said, "A few weeks after I left Royal, I realized I was late. I called you. Do you remember that?"

"Yes," he ground out. How could he forget? For four weeks, his pulse had leaped every time his phone rang. Only for his stomach to drop and his anger to rise when it turned out not to be her. So when her name had appeared on his screen, and her voice had caressed his ear, taunting him with its sultriness and sweetness that he could no longer have, he hadn't been welcoming. Hadn't been kind. "You mentioned nothing about being pregnant."

"No, but I tried. You didn't give me a chance to, because you had to go. A date that you couldn't be late for," she reminded him.

He'd lied; his ass had been planted on the couch in his sitting room at the ranch while he treated himself to his father's eighteen-year-old scotch. But his pride hadn't allowed him to admit that to her. He'd made up the date so she didn't know he hadn't been with a woman since she'd left him.

"Here's how you should've gone about that, Charlotte. 'Before you go, Ross, I'm pregnant.' Which, I repeat, you *didn't* do."

"No, I didn't," she replied, an edge honing her tone until it could slice clean through his sarcasm. "But I did try again. And when the call went straight to voice mail, I tried the ranch. The housekeeper told me you weren't home, but before I could hang up, she transferred me to Rusty. He demanded to know why I was attempting to contact you when I'd quit. I think…" She faltered, and this time, she did wrap her arms around herself and her gaze slid over his shoulder to the large window behind him. "I was so stunned that I just blurted out the truth about the pregnancy. He ordered me to get rid of the baby. That his son, an *Edmond*, would not end up raising a child with 'the help.'" Her lips twisted into a grim caricature of a smile, and his fingertips itched to rub those lips, smudge that ill-fitting smile from her mouth like faded lipstick. "He also told me he knew about our…relationship. Courtesy of you. And you'd assured him that you were done with me."

"That's a lie," he snarled, and her gaze jerked back to him. "I've never said anything to my father about us. I've never told anyone."

"Of course you haven't," she murmured, and those four words sent a slick, sour glide into his stomach.

"Dammit, Charlotte," he said, thrusting a hand through his dark blond hair, gripping the strands tight. "That's not how I meant it. I—"

"It was a long time ago, Ross," she interrupted, then

flicked a hand. "And whether or not he lied about that, he didn't about you moving on, did he?" She didn't wait for his answer but continued, "Anyway, he promised to have you contact me, but not before warning me that if I didn't go through with the termination of the pregnancy and breathed a word of it to anyone, he'd ruin me. And he wouldn't stop with just me, but he'd harm my parents, as well. I believed him."

"I can't believe..." But yeah...he did. His father would've been—was still—capable of doing all she'd relayed. He wouldn't have been above threatening an ex-employee to protect the precious Edmond name.

"Don't bother, Ross," she murmured, that bitter note making a reappearance. "You might be able to deny knowing about the phone call with Rusty, but you can't ignore the letter."

The letter. What letter?

Maybe she glimpsed the confusion in his eyes, because she scoffed, tipping her head back and muttering something toward the ceiling. Then she tugged her bag open and rummaged inside. Seconds later, she emerged with a worn, brown leather wallet. Opening it, she removed a folded piece of paper from the billfold and, crossing the short distance between them, slammed it onto his chest.

On reflex, he lifted his hand, covered hers. And that small contact—the first time he touched her in three years—nearly knocked him on his ass. Pleasure crashed into him, an anvil that had his fingers clasping hers, as if she were the one thing anchoring him to this world. His fingers flexed, starting to tighten around hers, needing to trap the burn from her palm that seemed to sear straight through to his skin.

But she snatched her hand back, retreating a step, leaving him clutching the paper. She cupped her palm, rubbing a thumb over it. Then, noticing that he caught the betraying action, she dropped her arms to her side.

"Do you want to read that aloud, Ross?" she asked, the rough silk of her voice a stroke over his chest, abdomen…lower. "Maybe it will jog your faulty memory."

He studied her closed-off expression but couldn't forget that telling gesture of hers…as if she were trying to erase the imprint of his touch. Not until the pointy edges of the paper bit into his fist did he glance down and slowly unfold it.

"Charlotte, you were intended to be a fling, not the mother of my child. Get rid of it. Use the enclosed check to pay for the procedure and your trouble. Then move on with your life, because I've moved on with mine. Russell Edmond Jr.," she recited the letter as he read it. "Russell Edmond Jr.," she repeated on a chuckle. "Like I no longer had the right to call you Ross. Nice touch."

Shock blasted him in an icy deluge. He damn near shattered with it.

"No," he breathed, rereading the paper for a second time. A third. Though typed, it was his signature. What *looked* like his signature. Because he damn sure hadn't written this, signed it or mailed it. "How…"

He knew the how. His father. Rusty had never mentioned a call with Charlotte, and he'd sent the letter, forged it.

Charlotte hadn't robbed him of the first two years of his son's life. Rusty had. Fury raged through him, an uncontrollable inferno desperate to destroy, to consume. And if his father had been in the building instead of attending an out-of-town meeting, Ross would've stormed down to his office and unleashed hell on him.

What a goddamn joke. He'd accused Charlotte of placing her needs above her son. Ross should've known better. After all, his father had been a prime example of a parent doing just that for years.

"You have no reason to believe me, Charlotte, but—" He cleared his throat of the thick snarl of emotion— the anger, the betrayal, the sadness—that lodged in his throat, and tried again. "But I didn't write this. I didn't even know where you lived in California to send it."

"It was mailed to my parents, who forwarded it to my sister, where I was staying. I kept the check, by the way," she supplied, her scrutiny like a magnifying glass determined to analyze every detail and nuance of his expression.

And he held nothing back—not the devastation over his father's lies. Not the grief over what they'd cost him. Not the pain of knowing she'd believed the worst of him. Yes, he might be guilty of being a man-whore, but not a deadbeat father. Not a poor excuse for a man, who would walk away from his responsibilities and ignore the existence of his child.

"I don't give a fuck about a check," he ground out, mind whirling a thousand miles a minute. "Why did you keep the letter?" he asked, holding it out to her, studying its perfectly folded edges that seemed permanently creased into the paper—as if it'd been opened and reread dozens of times. "Why are you carrying it around with you in your wallet?"

"As a reminder." She tugged the paper from his fingers and carefully refolded it, stowing it away in her purse before lifting her head and meeting his eyes. Resolved hardened her gaze. "Whenever I start to doubt myself, or am so tired I don't think I can go on, I pull this out and reread it. Remind myself that I did it once before, and I can do it again. Also, to remember that the only person I can truly count on is myself. Others might have failed me, but I refuse to do the same to myself."

"I didn't know, Charlotte," he murmured, that quiet but fierce statement a brutal blow to his chest. "I didn't know you were pregnant, and I never wrote you a letter telling you to get rid of my baby. I wouldn't…" He scrubbed a rough hand down his face. *I wouldn't abandon you, or my child.* Not after he'd been on the receiving end of that by his own mother. He understood the pain, the confusion, the sense of unworthiness. No, he wouldn't ever inflict that on another child, much less his own. "Give me a chance to prove to you that I can be a good father to Ben. A co-parent with you. I understand you don't owe me or my family anything, but I need you to give me a chance. Please, Charlotte."

She shook her head, and for the first time, indecision flickered across her face. "I—"

The door to his office swung open, and his sister strode in, frowning down at the tablet she held in her hand. "Ross, Valencia Donovan with Donovan Horse Rescue called. We need to send over—" She finally lifted her head, and spotting Charlotte first, jerked to a stop. "I didn't…" Gina glanced at Ross, then back at their ex-employee. "I'm sorry, Ross. Your assistant wasn't at her desk, so I just…" Her voice trailed off again, but with a small shake of her head, she gathered the poise and manners that had been instilled in her from the cradle. "Charlotte Jarrett. It's been a while," she greeted, walking toward Charlotte with her hand extended. "It's wonderful to see you again."

"Thank you," Charlotte enfolded Gina's hand in hers for a quick shake, before dropping it. The smile she summoned for his sister was small, weak. "It's good to be back home."

"Not to be nosy…" Gina grinned, shrugging a shoulder. "Forget that, I'm *definitely* being nosy. What're you doing here? Is your family okay?"

"Billy and I ran into her at Sheen a few nights ago. Charlotte's the new head chef there. I asked her to stop by and talk about hosting a tent at Soiree on the Bay, and possibly serving on the advisory board."

Gina smiled, nodding. "Wonderful. I've heard so many great things about Sheen and its new chef. I can't believe I didn't know it was you, Charlotte." She glanced down at her tablet again. "This can wait a little while, then. Could you find me after your meeting, Ross?"

"I can. Give me a few more minutes, and I'll come to your office."

"No need," Charlotte interrupted, and the desperation in her voice might not have been clear to his sister, but Ross caught it. "I need to get going anyway."

He almost objected; they weren't finished with their conversation, not by a long shot. But at the last moment, he swallowed the vehement protest, unwilling to draw undue attention to them. He wasn't ashamed of Ben— even now, he wanted to rent a billboard, post it on top of the Texas Cattleman's Club and declare to the world that he had a son. But this decision wouldn't affect just him, but also Charlotte and especially Ben. Until they hashed out details and he digested these new, earth-shattering revelations of the past, the information had to remain private.

"Oh, no. You don't have to leave on my account," Gina said, frowning.

"I'm not," Charlotte countered, though clearly she lied. Someone who'd just been pulled into a lifeboat off the sinking *Titanic* wouldn't have appeared more relieved than her. "It was nice seeing you again."

Gina crossed the short space separating them to grasp her elbow and give it a warm squeeze. "Same. And I'm so glad you're going to join us at Soiree on the Bay. You were a brilliant chef, and we'll be lucky to have you there. Welcome home, Charlotte."

"Thank you," she murmured. Barely sparing Ross a glance, she lifted a hand in a wave as she turned toward the office door. Her escape hatch. "Ross, I'll let you know about the advisory board position."

"I'll call you," he vowed, and they both knew he wasn't referring to the advisory board or the festival. He didn't care if it sounded ominous. If she tried to hide from him, or attempted to keep Ben from him, there were no lengths he wouldn't go to, to be in his son's life.

She nodded, then exited his office, pulling the door closed behind her.

"Are you sure I wasn't interrupting something more… personal?" Gina asked, her dark eyebrow arched high. Only his father failed to see and appreciate his sister's insightfulness and intelligence. Rarely did anything skate by her. Including the undercurrents of tension that fairly vibrated between him and Charlotte.

"No," he said, voice flat, inviting no further discussion on the topic. "Now what's going on with Valencia Donovan?"

Gina treated him to one last narrow-eyed scrutiny before diving into the reason behind her impromptu visit.

And Ross offered up a silent promise.

Charlotte might have escaped him for now.

But unlike three years ago, wherever she decided to go, he would damn well follow.

Five

"Well, the Hudsons can't stop raving about your food," Faith praised, strolling into Sheen's private dining room, from where Candice Hudson, her mother, aunt and several of their friends had just left, taking their excited chatter and laughter with them.

A glow of pleasure and satisfaction bloomed in Charlotte's chest as the restaurant manager sprawled in one of the chairs that Candice, the happy bride-to-be, and her party had just abandoned. Hearing that her food had been enjoyed never got old. Gathering up the last of the cards where the guests had scored the selection of food, she shot Faith a narrowed glance.

"Why are you so tired? I'm the one who did all the cooking, and the staff did the serving," she drawled.

The other woman waved a hand, flicking away her

tart words. "I had to talk. Do you know how exhausting it is to entertain and be *on*?" She sighed. "It's not a job for the weak."

Charlotte snorted, slipping the cards in the pocket of her chef's coat. "You poor, fragile thing."

"I know, right? But one must do what one must." Snickering, Faith jabbed a finger in Charlotte's direction. "But enough about me. The Hudsons just laid down a five-thousand-dollar catering deposit, and all because of your food. Not that I had any doubts that they wouldn't love your menu. Who could possibly resist grilled oysters with sweet basil, pesto and Parmesan? I swear, I just orgasmed saying that…"

"Oh, God, you're awful." Charlotte laughed, heading out of the private room and making a beeline for the kitchen. Faith followed, hot on her heels.

"What? They're aphrodisiacs. You're doing both the bride and groom a service for their wedding night."

"Stop it," Charlotte chided, even though she swallowed another burst of laughter. The first time Faith's naughty sense of humor had made an appearance, Charlotte had been in the middle of sampling a Parmesan lobster bisque. It hadn't been pretty. "I'm just glad they enjoyed what I put together."

The menu included additional food items for those guests who didn't like oysters or the balsamic and rosemary steak options. Coordinating the menu for the high-society wedding that would include nearly five hundred guests had been a challenge requiring hours of work. But the clients' obvious pleasure had been well worth the effort.

"*Loved* it," Faith corrected, trailing behind Charlotte into the bustling kitchen. "And the proud mother of the bride mentioned recommending us to all of her wealthy, connected friends for their wedding receptions and events. Now I have to speak with Jeremy about possibly printing out new brochures that focus on weddings and receptions. If the Hudsons are open to it, we could possibly hire a photographer to take some shots of their wedding and reception to spotlight in the pamphlets," she mumbled to herself, tapping away on her phone.

Switching her formal chef coat out for her work one, she washed her hands and left Faith to her notes and emails. Just as she moved to the stove to begin preparing the creamy wine sauce for her signature dish, the kitchen door opened and Jeremy Randall poked his head inside.

"Charlotte," he called, a tiny frown etching his brow. "Can I speak to you out here for a moment?"

"Sure." Inwardly sighing, she tossed a pining look at the stove and her ingredients. Faith hadn't been wrong. Entertaining people was exhausting, and after presenting each dish to the Hudsons and their guests, and explaining the ingredients in each one, all she longed for was to return to the kitchen and get lost in cooking. It was her happy place. But when the owner of the restaurant requested her presence, she couldn't refuse.

Seconds later, after instructions to her sous-chef to take over in her absence, she pushed through the kitchen door. It swung closed behind her and she joined Jeremy in the hall between the main dining area, the kitchen and prep area. "What can I do for you, Jeremy?"

The handsome older man ran a hand over his salt-and-pepper hair. With his smooth, unlined brown skin and tall, fit frame, Sheen's owner could've been anywhere between forty and sixty. The gray hair only lent a distinguished, composed air to his appearance. But right now, with his frown and the anxious gesture, he appeared more agitated than composed.

"Ah, Ross Edmond is here to see you."

Damn.

She should be surprised…but she wasn't. Ever since she'd left—okay, *bolted* out of—his office yesterday, she'd been expecting him to call her or turn up at her house as he'd done before. But not here at Sheen. She wasn't ready to field curious questions as to why the eldest son and heir to the Edmond Organization had an interest in her.

Out of habit, she reached for the necklace beneath her chef coat. She'd sent up so many prayers since her first and last encounter with Ross that he hadn't noticed its presence. How did she explain to him that she didn't want anything to do with him, wanted to erase him from her life, but she still wore the one gift from him that she'd allowed herself to keep? She'd thought she'd left it behind along with the other bracelets, earrings and clothes he'd purchased for her during their affair. And when she'd discovered it among her things in California, she'd almost thrown it out. But…she couldn't. Not when memories were attached to the gold chain and diamond-encrusted heart pendant like ghosts connected to an old house.

"I showed him into my office to give you a little privacy. But uh—" he cocked his head to the side, that dreaded curiosity glinting in his hazel gaze "—is there something I should know? Do you need me to stay with you?"

She shook her head, appreciative of his willingness to be her protective shield. But this battle was between her and Ross. "Not necessary. It's probably just about the tent for the Soiree on the Bay festival that I was telling you about," she said. "Nothing to worry about. But I shouldn't keep him waiting."

Although she wanted nothing more than to do just that.

"Okay, if you're sure," he said with a note of hesitation. "I'll be at the bar if you need me."

She nodded, and moments later, she twisted the knob to Jeremy's office and pushed it open. Ross's back faced the door, but as soon as she entered the room, he turned around, his startlingly blue gaze falling on her.

For a second, she froze. Because his crystal eyes, which were usually shuttered and guarded, were awash with anger and pain. God help her, but in that instant, she believed him about not writing the letter. And if she accepted that truth, then she also had to admit that he hadn't known about Ben, either. Those eyes…they didn't lie.

Where did that leave her? Well, she'd been trying to figure that out for the past twenty-four hours. Because three years of hurt and betrayal didn't just disappear overnight. She still didn't trust him—didn't trust that he would put Ben first over his family, put aside his lifestyle and make Ben a priority or take care not to trifle with her son's feelings.

Or her own.

She shut that thought down with a hard, open-handed slap. This wasn't about her; she had no claim on Ross other than him being Ben's father. Nor did she want one. Because he had shown her long ago that settling down with one woman wasn't what he desired. Especially not with her, a woman his father would never approve of.

She wasn't rich enough. Her parents weren't connected enough. Her pedigree didn't reach far back enough.

And she'd rebuffed Rusty's advances.

No, she was through hoping for the impossible with Ross. She was done three years ago, when he hadn't fought for her before she left Royal. It'd been her fault that she'd fallen in love with him knowing he could never offer that love in return.

She wouldn't be guilty of such blind devotion again.

"Ross," she said, shutting the door behind her. "What are you doing here at my job?"

"Tomorrow morning, I'm headed to Dallas for the next few days for meetings," he replied, his scrutiny flicking over her body before returning to her face. She convinced herself that her breasts didn't feel heavier, her belly didn't tighten and her sex didn't pulse from that cursory glance. She didn't feel *anything*. "I needed to settle things between us before I left. Charlotte—" the full, sensual curves of his mouth flattened before he continued, voice deepening "—I don't want any more time than necessary to pass by without me being in Ben's life or getting to know him. I've already lost so much of it."

"I—" She sighed, briefly closing her eyes. "I don't want you to, either, Ross."

"Then you believe me?" he pressed, shifting forward, his intense gaze hot on her face. "You believe that I didn't know about the phone call, the letter. About *Ben*."

"Yes," she murmured. "I do. But it doesn't change the fact that he doesn't know you. All he's ever known is me. We have to introduce you to him with care. I'm not going to disrupt his life or upset him."

Ross nodded. "I agree… Which is why I want him to live with me."

Horror and shock punched the breath from her lungs, and she could only stare at him. He intended to sue her for custody? Anger surged through her, a backdraft of emotion. And not just at him for planning to take her baby away from her. But at herself for actually believing he'd changed, that he wasn't selfish and self-absorbed any longer.

"I'm leaving," she said, turning away. There was nothing else for them to discuss—

"Dammit, wait," Ross growled, long fingers wrapping around her upper arm, drawing her to a halt. She tensed under his hand, hating the heat that radiated out from that firm grip. Hating that it seemed to brand every part of her. "I'm sorry. That came out wrong. Shit, Charlotte. I'm so far out of my depth here. Just… Just give me a minute."

Ross. *Apologizing?* She froze for an entirely different reason now. It was the apology and that frustrated, helpless note in his voice. Two things she'd never heard before from this confident, arrogant, charismatic man. It astonished her enough that she slowly pivoted, facing him again.

He released her, but her skin under her chef coat continued to throb as if his hand still clasped her.

"I don't want just Ben to live with me, Charlotte. I want you to move in with me, too."

Jesus, would he stop throwing verbal punches today? Just when she recovered from one, he opened his mouth and another plowed into her, pilfering her equilibrium.

"That's your idea of easing into this change?" she rasped, incredulous.

"Yes," he said. "Live together platonically as co-parents. So Ben can have you and me under one roof, raising him together."

"So, basically shacking up," she scoffed, shaking her head. "No, thank you."

"Charlotte—"

"No," she interrupted him. "Do you know what finding out I was pregnant and unmarried did to my relationship with my parents? Almost wrecked it. Healing that rift is part of the reason I returned to Royal. Now you want me to just obliterate all the progress we made by telling them I'm moving in with a man—with *you*? I won't do it."

Informing them that the heir to the Edmond Organization was the father of their grandson already promised to be one hell of an uncomfortable conversation.

"So we're supposed to live according to other people's views or opinions?" he challenged. "This is our son, not theirs."

"That's easy for you to say," she slung back. "You're Ross Edmond, Rusty's son. Heir to a fortune. No one would dare criticize or ostracize you. I can't live for myself, Ross. I have other people I'm responsible for, indebted to. And yes, I care about my parents' opinion. I'm not willing to lose them again."

"Fuck," he growled, thrusting a hand through his hair, tousling the ruthlessly styled strands. He paced away from her, halting in front of the far wall and staring at it for several long moments before whirling back around. "Charlotte, I feel like I'm clutching a handful of sand and it's steadily slipping through my fingers, no matter how tightly I hold on to it." He stretched his arm out, thrusting his fist forward, then peeling his fingers open, spreading them wide. "That's the years I've missed. The milestones I've lost. I can't get those back, and I'm trying so hard to grab on to the ones ahead of me. Every day that passes without me there is another day, another minute where something else could happen that I'll miss."

She blinked, taken aback by the vehemence, the *passion* in that plea. This man wanted his son. Wanted to be a part of his life. As a mother, as a woman with a heart, she couldn't deny him. Couldn't deny Ben, either. Because the truth was, although single mothers raised children all the time and did a damn fine job of it, there were things she couldn't teach Ben about manhood. There were things only his father or a male role model could. And while she loved having her father and brother-in-law in his life, they couldn't replace Ben's father.

She owed it to her baby boy to give Ross a chance to be a real father.

But move in with him?

She couldn't.

"I don't want to take that away from you, Ross," she murmured. "You should have every one of those moments, but…"

I can't compromise one more standard for you.

At one time in her life, she'd dreamed of living with Ross as his wife. Even when she'd called him three years ago, she'd still naively clung to that hope of being a family. Now what he offered was practically a marriage of convenience—without the benefit of marriage.

She was a single mother, and proud of it. But in the eyes of society, she would be the "baby mama" whom Ross screwed and knocked up. She refused to be the live-in woman who accepted his handout of a home but wasn't good enough to be "blessed" with his last name.

She had a line and couldn't cross it. Even though a part of her—that woman from three years ago who still clung to daydreams and impossible hope—yearned to not just cross it but leap over it.

"Don't say no just yet," Ross urged, erasing the distance between them with his sensual prowl. "Think about it for the couple of days I'm gone, and we can discuss it again."

She hesitated, then shrugged. "Okay, fine. I'll do that." Not that a couple of days would change her mind.

"Thank you."

He moved even closer, his arm lifting, that big hand hovering between them. Her breath snagged in her throat, and she stared at that so-damn-familiar hand with its short, buffed nails, long, elegant fingers and incongruously calloused palm. Ross might be a businessman and have possessed no interest in cattle ranching, but he'd loved horses. Sometimes it had seemed like he'd enjoyed their company more than people. That abraded palm appeared to testify that he still did. She also recalled how that skin used to feel against hers, that sensual contrast of rough and gentle, coarse and soft. A molten, sinuous warmth coiled around a jagged-edged lust, settling low in her belly. That was also how it had been between them.

Tender with teeth.

Just when she thought he would touch her, bring past

and present colliding together, he lowered his arm back to his side. Then slid that hand into his pants pocket as if he didn't trust it to behave if not landlocked.

"I'll call you tomorrow morning, if that's okay. Check in on Ben, at least say hi to him so he can start to become familiar with my voice."

She nodded. "That's fine."

Silence settled between them, as fragile and volatile as an undetonated bomb.

This is about Ben. This is about Ben.

The mantra marched through her mind, and she clung to it. Even as his sandalwood-and-earth scent embraced her, teasing her with the temptation of his big, powerful, sensually charged body. There'd been a time when she would've surrendered to that lure, cuddled against that tall frame and just inhaled his fragrance straight from the source of his sun-warmed skin. Let him cup her hip and the nape of her neck, press himself against her. Felt his cock nudge her stomach, promising her exquisite pleasure unlike anything she'd ever known.

Stifling a full-body shiver, she shifted backward, injecting desperately needed space between them. Space that didn't contain the memory of sex. Amazing, bone-melting, screaming-until-your-throat-was-raw sex.

"Talk to you soon," he said in that deep rumble of his that added more sensation to her imminent sensory overload.

She moved back and away, granting him room to exit the office. And only once the door closed did she exhale hard and loud.

Ross Edmond was trouble for her.

Some things never changed.

Six

Ross pulled his Aston Martin DBS to a stop in front of Elegance Ranch's scrolled, black iron gate. Pressing the automatic opener on his dashboard, he waited for it to part before driving through to the circular drive. He paused, his nearly soundless engine idling while he stole a moment to stare beyond the palatial Palladian-style villa to the setting sun. Beams of gold, deep orange and brilliant red streamed across the rich ranchland and rolling fields, transforming the estate into a beautiful world that appeared to be on fire.

This was his favorite time of day. For some, it was morning when the day loomed rich with possibilities. But for him, it was evening. It meant a day of hard work, accomplishments and completed goals. It meant a sense of satisfaction that he'd pulled his weight, been a man, not just an Edmond. And the beauty of the sunset congratulated him.

Sighing, he slowly drove into the air-conditioned multicar garage, and after switching the ignition off, just sat there inside the car's plush interior. A quiet peace filled him at being back home after three days in Dallas. Meetings and dinners had filled those hours, for both the Edmond Organization and the festival business. Everything had gone well, and pride filtered through him. Even his father couldn't complain about the connections and headway he'd made. Well, Rusty Edmond actually could find something to criticize, because that was what he did.

Speaking of Rusty...

Clenching his jaw, Ross shoved the car door open. For days he'd put off this conversation with his father because it wasn't one he'd wanted to have over the phone. He needed to look into Rusty's eyes, see each nuance and tick of his expression as Ross confronted his father about lying to him for three years about Charlotte.

Rage that had simmered at times, but never fully extinguished, flared to a flash fire as he exited the garage. Each step through the sprawling and luxurious home stoked those flames. This time of evening, his father would be in one place—his study. Sipping on a tumbler of whiskey before settling in to continue the work he hadn't finished at the office.

For as long as Ross remembered, work had been his father's obsession. Well, work and women. A man couldn't marry four times and not make room for play. But each marriage had ended because he treated his wives the same way he did his children. Like employ-

ees. There for his instruction, censure and disposal.
And very rarely his praise.

When any of those wives dared complain, he'd sweep
an arm out as if inviting them to look around them. Telling them that the work they nagged about had bought
the estate, with its many rooms for entertaining, bedrooms and private baths, resort-style pool, stables,
several guesthouses and miles and miles of ranchland.
Moreover, his many hours at the office paid for the
designer clothes, purses and jewelry in their walk-in
closets and the extravagant parties they threw on the
entertainment pavilion.

Yes, Rusty Edmond could be an arrogant, sarcastic dick.

Which, again, explained the four ex-wives.

On his way to Rusty's study, Ross passed the state-
of-the-art kitchen with its separate service kitchen, but-
ler's pantry and wine cellar. It didn't require exerting
too much imagination to remember Charlotte rushing
around in there, owning the area like the pro she was.
That was how she'd first nabbed his attention. That
confidence. That cool poise in the midst of controlled
chaos. That wild beauty.

And those quick, clever hands.

Shit, did it make him a pervert that those hands so easily and assuredly chopping vegetables, stirring sauces,
flipping meat or skillfully plating exquisite dishes had
hardened his cock so it resembled the marble floor in the
entryway? So delicate, so fine-boned, but strong and capable. He couldn't watch her sauté food and not visual-
ize those fingers wrapped with the same dexterity and
talent around his dick.

It hadn't just been her flagrant curves and gorgeous face that had drawn him to her like a moth to a flame. He'd been surrounded by beautiful women since before his balls dropped. But Charlotte had possessed… something more. To this day, he couldn't put his finger on it. But whatever that "something" was, it'd captured him…hell, *enraptured* him. Whereas other women had been transient, he returned time and again to her. Unable to stay away. Unable to satisfy that hungry hole that only being with her had seemed to fill.

Then she'd left.

But it had been his father who'd kept her out of his life.

His father who had prevented him from knowing his son.

His father who *owed* him.

Ross didn't knock on the closed door of Rusty's study but twisted the knob and entered. His father, still in a light gray dress shirt, barely glanced up from his desk, sparing Ross a narrowed look before returning his focus to the computer.

"You're back," he said in that booming, deep voice that could issue curt orders and deliver charming compliments whenever the occasion warranted. "Sometime between when you left and now, did you leave your manners in Dallas? A closed door usually means you knock and wait to be admitted."

"Sorry," Ross said, without the faintest hint of sincerity. Which his father must've noted, because he shifted his wintry gaze away from the monitor to settle on him. "I need to talk to you."

"I'm in the middle of something. It'll have to wait."

"No. Now."

His father's big frame stiffened, and for several seconds they stared at one another, adversaries engaged in a visual battle. Usually, Ross would be the first to look away, to end the pissing contest that always struck him as macho bullshit.

But not today.

Maybe his father sensed this, because the corner of his mouth lifted in a smirk as he leaned back in his massive black leather chair that more resembled a throne than office furniture.

"Well, if you insist, son," Rusty drawled, arching an eyebrow and sweeping a hand toward the visitor chairs in front of his desk. "Sit."

Like a dog.

But with fury rumbling and festering inside him like an angry, infected wound that needed to be lanced, he wasn't in the mood to heel.

He strode closer to his father, ignoring the chairs and coming to a halt directly in front of the massive glass desk. "Have you been to Sheen yet?"

"The restaurant?" He frowned. "No. What's this shit? You have your balls in a sling over food?"

That was his father. All class.

"Then you don't know who the owner hired as executive chef?" Ross pressed, ignoring the vulgar question.

"No, Ross, I don't know," his father growled. "Since it's not putting money in my pocket, I don't really give a damn who the cook is."

"Chef," Ross corrected. "And it's Charlotte Jarrett, Dad. Charlotte is the new chef."

An emotion too quick to identify flickered in his father's gaze before it shuttered. Rusty had created and patented the poker face. He only displayed what he desired anyone to see. And right now his expression was as shut tight as one of the infamous NDA clauses he demanded of his lovers.

"Charlotte Jarrett," he repeated, voice cold and flat. "I had no idea she'd returned to town."

"Yes, she has."

"So? What does that have to do with either of us? She was an employee years ago. Staff has come and gone from this place before, and I never made it my business to keep track of them. Why should it interest me?"

"Is this the game you want to play?" Ross murmured, not surprised in the least. He hadn't expected his father to admit what he'd done. Rusty considered himself a master chess player, and not just on the board, but in life. He would allow his opponent to make their move so he could counter, evade or trap. "Okay, fine. Have it your way." He cleared his throat, then prepared for battle. "Well, three years ago, after Charlotte quit, she called here looking for me but got you instead."

Rusty didn't respond, just continued to stare at him with that unwavering gray stare. Silently daring him to proceed.

Ross shoved down the rage, covering it with a sheet of ice. He refused to hand his father ammunition to use against him, to turn around and accuse him of being irrational. "She told you about her relationship with me."

"You mean, she told me you two were fucking."

Those red-and-orange-tinged flames licked at his gut. Enticing him to let this consuming anger loose. *It's what he wants. I'm not giving him what he wants.*

"But that wasn't the only thing, was it?"

Again, no answer from Rusty. But the slight flare of his nostrils, the even slighter thinning of his mouth telegraphed his annoyance.

"She was pregnant. And you told her to get rid of it. Get rid of my baby," Ross ground out.

"So?"

You can't hit your father. You can't hit your father.

The mantra spilled through his head, and Ross silently repeated it several more times before he was fully convinced that he couldn't take that course of action.

"So," he echoed coldly. "You told her to get rid of *my* baby. *Not yours.* You had no right."

Rusty snorted. "The hell I didn't. You're my son, and I wasn't allowing some random girl to trap you."

"And that baby is *my son*," Ross threw back. "You didn't even tell me about him, didn't give me the opportunity to make a choice that was mine, not yours."

"What the fuck do you mean—*is my son*?" Rusty asked, voice soft, dangerous, eyes narrowing.

"Yeah, Dad." Ross nodded, scalding satisfaction flooding him. "*Is.* As in Charlotte didn't do what you ordered her to do in that phone call or that phony-ass letter you sent with my forged signature." Disgust churned inside him. "Despite all your manipulations, she had my baby. My son."

"How do you know, Ross?" Rusty demanded, slowly rising from his chair. He planted his fists on his desk, leaning forward.

"Because I've seen him. Met him."

"You're fucking lying," his father snarled, pounding a fist on the glass desktop. "She didn't have that baby."

"Yes, she did." Ross smiled, and not with a small amount of pride. Charlotte had done what he, himself, had found difficult to do. Stood up to and defied the great and mighty Russell Edmond Sr. "For once, someone didn't obey your edicts. And he's absolutely mine."

"Why? Because some loose-legged girl who you fucked says so? If she opened her legs so easily for you, Ross, who else did she give it up for? Use your head, not your dick."

"Watch yourself," Ross growled. "You don't get to talk about her like that."

"What? She's your supposed 'baby mama' and now you're her champion?" Rusty chuckled, the sound mean, dirty. Because his father didn't know how to fight any other way but down in the mud. "She was the *help*, son. And if you think she didn't see you as a ripe opportunity to climb into a world she has no business in, then you're a goddamn idiot. She was a user then, and she's one now if she's showing up out of the blue with a kid and trying to pawn it off on you. Do you really believe you were the first one she tried to get under? I promise, you weren't."

"Last time, Dad," he warned, steel threading his voice. "Keep your mouth shut about her. And Ben is mine. I had a DNA test done. And despite your best intentions, I'm claiming my son and intend to get to know him."

"The hell you are," Rusty snarled. "I refuse to allow you to tarnish this family's name by having anything to do with this woman and her baby."

"Get used to it." Ross mimicked his father's pose, flattening his hands on the desk and leaning forward so only inches separated them. "Because I've asked Charlotte to move into the ranch with me. Her and Ben. I'm going to be a father to my son whether you like it or not."

"I forbid it, Ross. This is what she wants, what she wanted when she called up here looking for you years ago. Don't you see that? You're upset about the letter I sent her? Well, did she happen to mention the check I included? Ten thousand dollars, son. And she cashed the check. Wake up, Ross, she's just a gold digger."

Ross barked out a harsh crack of laughter. "Is that supposed to mean something? Am I supposed to look down on her for that? She was a soon-to-be single mother who'd left everything behind—her family, her home, her job. You really believe I begrudge her using that check for whatever she needed to care for herself and our son?" He shook his head. "And gold digger? That name doesn't exactly apply since she hasn't asked me for a damn cent in three years."

She's not my mother, hovered on the tip of his tongue. She hadn't abandoned her child, taken the money and ghosted out of his life. Charlotte might have walked away from Ross, but not their son. He granted her major points for that. "It's happening, Dad. She hasn't agreed yet, but it's only a matter of time."

"Not under my roof. And let's not pretend that this house, this land, this company, hell, your *life*, aren't mine. I own all of it. The lifestyle of cavorting off to different cities around the world to do whatever the hell you want without a care? That's courtesy of me. The expensive suits and watches you like to flash? Me. All me. And if you go through with this…idiocy of claiming this woman's son, of trying to move her in here, there will be repercussions. Repercussions you literally can't afford to deal with. Don't force my hand on this, Ross. Cut ties with her and this boy. And cut ties *now*."

"Two years," Ross whispered, deliberately straightening, his gaze never leaving his father's.

"What?" Rusty snapped.

"Two years. That's how old my son is. Two years of not knowing he existed. Two years of firsts. Two years of his life that you stole from me. From us. Do your worst, Dad. Issue your threats. But you don't get another day, another hour."

"Goddammit, Ross—"

"Hey, fellas." Ross turned around in time to see Billy shut the study door behind him and walk farther into the room frowning. "I could hear you two all the way down the hall. And so can the staff. What's going on?" He cast a look from Ross to Rusty, then back to Ross, concern darkening his eyes. "Is everything okay?"

"Hell no, everything isn't okay," Rusty growled. "Talk to your friend, Billy. See if you can pound some sense into him, because I can't seem to. But somebody better," he threatened.

"Ross—" Billy said.

"Later," he threw at his friend before tossing a look at his father over his shoulder. "We'll finish this later."

"No, we won't. Don't push this, Ross."

"No, don't push *me*, Dad."

Stalking across the study, he jerked the door open and left, the anger, disappointment and, yes, sadness, propelling him down the hall toward the steps that led to the second level and his wing of the house. He'd expected his father's reaction. But he hadn't been prepared for Rusty to deny a child—to urge Rusty to desert a child—that was their blood. All Ross's life, Rusty had preached about teaching his son to "be a man." But a man took care of his responsibilities, provided for his children. A man protected the vulnerable.

Though Ross and his father had their differences, he'd always seen his father as a man upholding those values.

Now the sadness inside him threatened to capsize the anger. The sadness for who he'd believed his father to be. For the death of that belief.

"Ross, what the hell?" A hard grip surrounded his upper arm, drawing him to an abrupt halt. Billy appeared in front of him, blocking his path to the staircase. "What's going on?" Before Ross could answer, his friend guided him through the formal living room on their left and out the glass French doors that led to one of the terraces facing the stables. Once they were several feet away from the house and on the lighted, pebbled path, he stopped, thrusting his hands over his black hair. "Talk to me. What the hell happened in there with Rusty?"

Initially, Ross hadn't any intention of talking about Charlotte and Ben with anyone. At least not until his temper cooled. But the story burst out of him on a ragged, streaming torrent. When he finished, his chest rose and fell on his harsh breaths and the maelstrom of emotions that continued to roil through him.

"Well, damn," Billy murmured. "I wasn't expecting all that."

For the first time since entering his father's study,

Ross snorted with true humor. "Yeah, when it comes to drama, I'm all go big or go home." But in the next instant, he sobered. "Just tell me what you're thinking, Billy."

His friend sighed. "I don't agree with how your father handled the situation those years ago. Lies always end up hurting everyone in the end. But trying to see it from his point of view, I can understand his motives—"

"Are you *serious*?" Ross barked. "He kept this—"

"Hold up." Billy thrust up a hand. "I said I could understand his motives, not that I agree with them. Ben is your son, and no man should ever walk away from his child. I like your father, respect him, but I can't back him on this. You're my friend, and whatever you need, I got you."

Love and gratitude for this man, who was as close to him as his brother, Asher, filled Ross, soothing the jagged edges left behind by the argument with his father.

"I appreciate it, Billy," he said, then exhaled roughly. "I'm going to need all the moral support I can get. Especially when this comes out. Because I refuse to hide Ben or Charlotte."

"You mean you're going to need all the support because of Rusty."

"Yes," Ross murmured. "Why does it feel like I'm about to go to war with my father?"

"He'll calm down," Billy assured him, clapping a hand to his shoulder. "Right now he's upset, but once he calms down, he'll see reason."

Ross chuckled sadly. "You don't know Rusty Edmond at all, do you?"

Because *he* did. Rusty didn't forgive or forget. And

Ross had openly defied him, when in the past all he'd had was his son's obedience.

No, this wouldn't blow over. Not when neither of them were ready to back down.

But this was one battle Ross couldn't afford to lose.

Seven

This time as Ross approached the small house in the older but cozy section of Royal, he was expected. He'd called Charlotte as soon as he'd hit the city limits last evening to let her know he was back in town. And asked if he could drop by the following morning to see Ben.

Over the three days that he'd been in Dallas, he'd called and talked to her, and had even video-chatted with Ben over his phone. Not that a two-year-old could chat. But he had been able to coax a *hi* out of him. Those moments had carried him through the long, interminable three days. And one day, hopefully sooner rather than later, his son would smile when he saw Ross's face and heard his voice. Would run to Ross when he saw him.

God, he lived for that day.

Butterflies. He'd never experienced butterflies in

his stomach before. The closest had been the tightening and twisting of his gut when he'd known he would be with Charlotte. But that had been about anticipation, desire. Not nerves. No, these were honest-to-God nerves. And not over a woman, but for a boy. A toddler who had the power to squeeze his heart so hard that the ache throbbed in his chest.

Climbing the shallow steps to the front door, he dragged in a breath, then knocked. Within seconds, the door opened as if the person on the other side had just been waiting on him.

Charlotte stood in the entryway, her dark hair hanging in a long braid over her shoulder. A long-sleeved, emerald dress clung to her full breasts before the soft material fell to the floor. She looked casual, even comfortable. But there was nothing comfortable about how his cock thumped against his zipper, stretching, hardening. Dammit. The woman could make a nun's habit sexy as fuck.

"Hi, Ross," she greeted, stepping back, granting him room to enter. "Come on in."

"Thanks." Instead of studying the elegant slant of her cheekbone or the sensual curve of her mouth or—hell—the lush rise of her breasts, he surveyed her home. As if it were his first time there. As if he hadn't memorized every square footage of the place that he'd seen. Anything was better than staring at her like a starved animal.

Hell, he shouldn't find her sexy. Shouldn't want her. Shouldn't fucking *feel* around her.

He accepted she hadn't lied to him or kept his son away from him out of spite or malice, but he still didn't trust her. Didn't trust her not to disappear—she'd done it once before. He also didn't trust her not to renege on allowing him access to Ben.

But while he might be angry—an *understatement*—with his father, Rusty Edmond had still raised him. And one thing he'd taught Ross was to understand what your opponent needed and find a way to supply it. It might seem inherently wrong that he viewed Charlotte as his adversary, but right now he wanted her and Ben to live with him, and she was opposed to the idea. So he'd found her weakness and was prepared to lean on it until she surrendered. She'd shown him that he wasn't enough for her to stick around for. Maybe his incentive *would* be.

Fighting fair? No. Was he being his father's son at the moment? Probably.

Did he care? Not even a little bit.

"Where's Ben?" he asked, glancing toward the living room.

"My parents have him. I usually run later than usual on Friday nights, and they offered to keep him until this morning. They're bringing him home shortly."

Disappointment coalesced inside his chest, tight and hot.

"I texted you last night to let you know, just in case you wanted to drop by later this morning," she said, her tone apologetic.

"Yeah, I didn't see it." In his haste to confront his father as soon as he got back, he'd forgotten his phone in the car, and hadn't checked it for messages yet when he'd retrieved it today. "Maybe this works out better. We can talk over some things before he gets here."

She stared at him, then slowly dipped her head. "Fine." Without waiting for him, she strode toward the living room, and he followed. She didn't sit on the couch or love seat but turned and faced him. The resolute jut of her chin and the thrust of her hip relayed that he didn't have an easy battle ahead of him.

He hadn't expected it to be.

"I spoke with Billy while I was in Dallas," he said, starting with a more innocuous subject. "He told me you agreed to serve on the festival advisory board."

"Yes. I brought it to Jeremy, Sheen's owner, and Faith Grisham, the manager, and they both agreed it would be in the restaurant's best interest to host a tent and for the head chef to be on the board. Billy assured me the meetings wouldn't interfere with my work schedule. And as long as they don't take up too much of my time with Ben, I'm willing to do it."

"We appreciate it. Whatever input and ideas you can add will be valuable. Thank you for doing this, Charlotte."

She shrugged a shoulder and unfolded her arms. Skimming a hand over her braid, she huffed out a breath. "We'll see how it works out," she said, and then added, "Rip the Band-Aid off, Ross. You want my answer about moving in with you, and it's still the same as it was before. No, I can't."

"Hear me out first, Charlotte," he requested, shifting closer to her, and after a second, slid his hands in his suit pockets. That was becoming a habit when around her. Occupying or trapping his hands so they didn't rebel and do something heinous like run the backs of his fingers over the delicate but stubborn line of her jaw. Trail his fingertips over the lush curve of her bottom lip. Grab that braid, fist it and tug her head back...

Fuck.

Refocusing, he gazed into her brown eyes and proposed the arrangement that he'd been formulating over the last three days.

"I understand your reservations about moving in with me. Especially given our...past. But I have a counteroffer." The rough thudding of his heart belied the calm of his voice. He *needed* her to agree. But pride kept him from letting her know that. In his experience, voicing what you wanted, *begging for it*, had zero effect. The one time he had, his mother had walked away and left him and Gina anyway. It'd been the best and the cruelest lesson he'd learned. "Commit to one year of you and Ben living with me. Just one so I can get to know my son, and we can work out how to co-parent. Then if, at the end of the year, you decide it's not working, you can leave."

When she didn't say anything, he risked moving closer, and that sharp and sweet scent teased him with a heavier, spicier fragrance. One that had to do less with figs and sugar and was more raw, pure woman.

Fuck if he didn't hunger to lap it off her smooth hickory skin.

"Also, at the end of the year," he continued, centering his attention once more on the conversation and not how delicious she used to taste, "I'll gift you with five hundred thousand dollars to go toward anything you desire—like maybe opening your own restaurant. I remember that was your dream."

He'd anticipated surprise or even a token resistance

before quick capitulation. But he hadn't predicted the indignation simmering in her dark eyes.

"A bribe?" she bit out. "That's your counteroffer? Your solution to the problem I represent? Throw money at me?"

"It's not a bribe—"

"Right," she drawled, her tone so sharp it sliced through the thick tension crowding the room. "It's a *gift*. Like the ones you used to leave in the guesthouse for me to find. Or the ones you undoubtedly give all the other women you sleep with and don't bother to call. Same sentiment, different dollar amount. No, thanks. I don't need your guilt gifts."

Anger surged inside him, joined by a scalding hot retort to her unfair accusation. Hell, he'd been trying to give her what she wanted, and she was…damn, she was *right*. Realization doused the flames. He blinked at her, and for the first time, he glimpsed himself in her eyes.

It was true. While they were together, he'd think nothing of having his secretary purchase the latest, most expensive purse or shoes. Or have his jeweler send over a glittering pair of earrings, ring or bracelet. The gifts had been an afterthought, nothing to him. And after her, he'd done the same with the parade of women who'd graced his arm, his bed. None of them had ever complained when he sent jewelry and a note of thanks for a wonderful night.

It wasn't meant as a demeaning or dismissive gesture; it was…what he knew. He'd witnessed his father do it time and time again with his wives and girlfriends, and it'd appeased them, momentarily healing the rift between them and Rusty.

Even his mother had taken a hefty divorce settlement and left, happy to go about her way without her family in her daily life.

Yet the explanation lodged in his throat. At one time in their relationship, he might have been able to share this with Charlotte. Like after the scent of sex perfumed the air of her bedroom, the sheets tangled around their sweat-dampened bodies as she lay sprawled over him, her breath tickling his chest. Back then, in those quiet soul-baring moments when they'd shared their hopes and dreams, disillusionments and disappointments, he could've admitted this revelation of how he used money as emotional currency.

But not now.

"I'm sorry," he said, his mind whirring to find the words to convey his sincerity while struggling to convince her not to abandon this plan. "I didn't mean to offend you, Charlotte. I was only thinking that other than your job at Sheen, you would be rearranging your life for an entire year for me, the least I could do was help you achieve what you've always wanted. It's only a gift. Whether you stay or you leave, the money is yours."

She didn't immediately reply but simply stared at him. Finally, she glanced away, murmuring something he couldn't catch under her breath.

"And after a year, Ross?" she asked quietly, returning her scrutiny to him. "What then? Do we just walk away from the little experiment as if it didn't happen? Do we pretend we haven't let Ben become accustomed to a certain living arrangement where he has both parents every day in his life to separate houses again with biweekly visits?" She sighed, shaking her head, her gaze sad. "What about you? After being a father every day, how do you handle going to only seeing him a few times a week? Have you thought about how that will affect you?"

Again, she stunned him.

By broaching another aspect he hadn't considered, but also because she was concerned…about him.

"I hadn't thought about that," he admitted gruffly. Narrowing his gaze on the neat stack of toys across the room, he swallowed past his suddenly constricted throat. "For me, I'd rather have that year where I wake up to Ben and have the privilege of putting him to bed. Where I can feed him breakfast, can experience his good and bad moods, his smiles and frowns…hear him call me Daddy. I'd rather have twelve months of that even knowing there's a possibility that I might not have it in exactly that way afterward."

She glanced away from him, and her slender throat worked before she returned her attention back to him. "And what about Ben?" she whispered.

Ross studied her for a long moment. "You're a wonderful mother—I can tell that from being with him those ten minutes. Hopefully, you can teach me to be an equally great father. And between the two of us, I know we can help him navigate and adapt to any change. He needs to know me, Charlotte," he said, voice lower, rawer, exposing the depths of his emotion. "And I need to know him."

He didn't voice it, but he assumed that at the end of the twelve months, she would want to leave. But what if she *didn't*? What if she discovered she enjoyed a more luxurious life at the ranch where she didn't have to worry about bills, expenses or day care? They could go on indefinitely with the living arrangement. Hell, even a…marriage, maybe. Bottom line? They could essentially live separate lives but still be a family for Ben.

But he needed her to say yes first before bringing that option to the table.

"Jesus, I can't believe I'm actually considering this," she muttered, and the low grumble most likely not meant for his ears had a cautious joy and sweet satisfaction pulsing through his veins. "*If* I agree to this, I have a couple of conditions."

He risked a nod.

"One, I'm not moving to your family's estate." When he frowned, she shook her head. Hard. "No. I'm not compromising on that. I won't be under your father's roof. I've worked too hard to be independent, and I won't give that up to be reliant on you or Rusty."

"Where would we stay then?" he asked, glancing around her living room. What he'd seen of her home was nice, but the house was small. "How many bedrooms do you have?"

"Two."

He shook his head. "I'm not saying no to this condition. But would you concede to us looking for another place together? I don't want to confiscate Ben's room, and then he'll have to move into your room. That's not fair to either of you."

She studied him for a moment, then finally, she nodded. "Okay, I can concede to that."

"And you're renting, right?" When she dipped her head again, he said, "I'll cover the rest of the rent that's left on your lease. No, Charlotte, I'm *insisting* on that," he growled as her lips parted, undoubtedly to object. "It's because of me and what I'm asking you to do that you're moving in the first place. It's the least I could do."

She sighed and grudgingly muttered, "Fine."

"What's your second condition?" he asked, anxious to get all her concerns out there so he could tackle them one by one.

"I'm not accepting your money or *gift*," she added.

"No." This time he shook his head, vehemently. "For two years, you've provided for Ben on your own without any financial help from me. If I'd known about him, I would've gladly paid child support. Consider this a lump sum of back payments. The money is yours and Ben's, Charlotte. I'm not negotiating on this."

Again she hesitated, but eventually nodded. "Okay. That's fair."

"Good. Now *I* have one last condition." He paused. "I want Ben to have my last name."

He braced himself for her argument, had his reasons ready—he was, after all, Ben's father; if he'd been at the birth, he would've signed the birth certificate; and he wanted to claim his son.

But shock erupted inside him, stealing those words and his breath when she whispered, "Okay."

"Thank you," he said softly.

They stared at one another, and the tension vibrating between them thickened, tightened to the point of bursting. As if of its own volition, his gaze dropped to her mouth, and he could practically feel the softness of it. The tender give of it. The gut-twisting greediness of it.

Fuck, he wanted it. Wanted it all. That uninhibited response to him that held no artifice. That needy moan he remembered so well he could hear a faint echo of it now. That sultry, addictive taste that'd had him counting down the hours until he could see her again. Indulge in her again. *Devour* her again.

He'd never been one to deny himself. And he didn't now.

Lust throbbing in his veins, he edged closer, eliminating the space between them. Immediately, the heat from her body and the rich, heady perfume from her skin inundated him, and he inhaled. It was visceral. Intoxicating. Borderline...sexual. Taking a part of her into him, just as he'd once slid so hard and deep inside her.

He granted her time to move, to avoid him—at least he convinced himself he did. And when she didn't, just stared up at him with those lovely, bottomless eyes, he surrendered to the urge that had been riding him since the moment he'd seen her cross that restaurant floor, her sexy, confident stride carrying her to his table.

Need was a growling, straining animal inside him, but he didn't pounce on her like that beast demanded. Not when it had been three years of deprivation, of starving for the touch that taunted him in his most secret, dirtiest dreams.

Because it had been that long, he intended to *savor*.

Dragging his fingertips up the elegant column of her neck, he relished the softness of her skin before tunneling his fingers under her braid and over her scalp. Her low, soft gasp bathed his lips as he lowered his head, and when he took her mouth, he took that small, hungry sound, as well.

He groaned as his lips closed over hers, unable to restrain it. Not when her lips parted for him so sweetly, as if she didn't resent every breath he drew. As if this need wasn't one-sided. As if she'd been dying for a taste of him, too.

He slid his tongue over that overripe bottom lip, sucking on it for good measure before slipping between. Slipping into heaven. Into *her*. With another moan, he pressed closer, aligning his larger frame against her curvier one. God, she was made for him. Even as the thought prowled through his head, he hated it, shoved it aside so hard it ricocheted off his skull. Sentimental drivel had no place here. Not when her tongue greeted his, lapped at his, tangled with his.

This. He lifted his other hand, cupping her cheek, holding her for a deeper, harder possession. *This* was what he'd been searching for the last three years with the nameless, faceless parade of women. This hit, like an unhealthy combination of dopamine and alcohol, arrowed straight to his system. That lethal mix pumped through his arteries, aided by his wildly hammering heart, and pounded in the erect thickness of his cock.

One kiss. She had him on the verge of coming with *one* kiss.

He angled her head, positioning her so he could take more. No, to hell with that. *Conquer* more. He wanted to brand her with his kiss so she would remember clearly how he made her body convulse with pleasure, made her throat raw by eliciting scream after scream.

He could do that for her now. Fuck, he *needed* to do that for her now. For him, too.

She released a whimper then leaned her head back, turning to the side. "Ross," she rasped.

He trailed his damp lips over her cheek to her ear.

There, he pressed a kiss to the tip and murmured, "Come away with me this weekend."

The invitation tumbled from his lips before the idea had fully formed. A warning alarm blared in his head, loud and screaming, What the fuck? But he didn't rescind the offer. Though she stiffened against him, he didn't release her, just shifted his hand from her face to her hip, steadying her.

"I have a cabin in Colorado. You, Ben, me—we can fly there tonight after you're finished at the restaurant, spend tomorrow there, and I'll have you back Monday in time for work. We can talk over the details of the move and how we're going to proceed with our families. I want to spend time getting to know my son with his mother. Take a risk and a day off work, Charlotte."

"I don't have to take a day off," she murmured, almost absently. "One of my conditions when I accepted the job at Sheen was that I have Sundays off to be with Ben."

Whether she realized it or not, she was halfway to agreeing to go with him. He pushed his advantage, because the invite might've been spontaneous, but he wanted this. Wanted her and Ben alone.

"Say yes, Charlotte," he said, finally stepping back even though his body screamed in rebellion and promised swift retribution. Even though his palms tingled with the need to cup that rounded, firm hip again. To squeeze it. Mark it. "This is about Ben. What happens afterward—*if* something happens—is up to you."

Her eyes darkened, and the thick fringe of her lashes lowered. But not before he caught the gleam of arousal in her eyes. The uncertainty, too. Yes, she'd understood his meaning. He hadn't been referring to their co-parenting plan or how they intended to break the news to her parents that he was Ben's father.

He'd meant that kiss.

And the hot, raw sex that followed.

When he'd proposed their…cohabitation, he'd stipulated it would be platonic. And that had been his plan. Up until she'd moaned into his mouth.

Now he was leaving it up to her; the ball was in her court. And if she wanted to play, he was all in. A year with free access to her body, to her pleasure?

He wanted it. He wanted *her*.

Trust her? No. Dying to be buried inside her? Hell. Yes.

"Come away with me." The offer, roughened by the lust tearing at him, still hung between them.

Her lips parted, moved, but nothing emerged. She bowed her head, pinching the bridge of her nose. Anticipation and the need to press for an answer whipped inside him like a gathering summer storm, but he held back. Granting her space and time to come to her decision. Because it had to be hers, freely given.

Finally, she lifted her head, met his gaze. Desire still simmered in her eyes as did the doubt. But so did resolve. He had his answer even before she murmured, "Yes."

He exhaled. "Good," he said. "Call me when you're about to leave work. I'll come by to pick up you and Ben tonight."

"Okay." She sighed. Then whispered, "I hope we're not making a mistake, Ross."

The assurance that they were doing the right thing

hovered on his tongue, but he couldn't utter it. Because it would be a lie.

He didn't know.

And right now, he didn't care.

Eight

A cabin, he said.

Charlotte shook her head, smiling wryly down into the steaming cup of coffee she cradled between her palms.

Only Ross Edmond would call this luxurious four-story chalet in exclusive Telluride, Colorado, a cabin. She scoffed. *Right*. And Godzilla was a cute little lizard with anger issues.

Leaning on the wood railing, she studied the beauty of Mount Wilson and sipped the fragrant brew. Somehow the coffee tasted better up here in the mountains, with the crisp air biting at her cheeks. It should've been too cold to stand outside, but bundled up in her oversize sweater and a coat Ross provided from one of the cabin's fully stocked closets, and with the freestanding fireplace at her back, she was warm enough.

And even if she'd been in danger of frostbite, she still would've remained out here on this ridiculously gorgeous terrace, watching her son and his father play together.

Ben had gone a little crazy at the sight of snow; he'd never experienced it in California, and though it did fall in Texas, none had fallen since they'd returned to Royal. His excited squeal had filled her chest with joy, and even if she was questioning her wisdom in agreeing to this impromptu trip, that delighted and wondrous sound had silenced every misgiving.

Ross had always appeared to her as self-confident. Arrogant. So sure of himself. But from the moment he had picked them up from her house, through the drive to the airport and the trip here in the Edmonds' private jet, he'd been different. Uncertain. Even a little bit… nervous. And she knew the reason why.

Ben.

The small, three-foot-tall boy had humbled Ross Edmond.

He was in awe of Ben, and the fascination seemed mutual. Between the phone calls over the days Ross had been in Dallas and the trip here, Ben had lost most of his shyness, and had been stuck like glue to Ross. Falling asleep in his arms on the flight here. Climbing on his lap and contentedly eating with his father. And now building a really abysmal-looking snow fort in the huge yard behind the chalet.

They had a real bromance going on.

One of Ross's reasons for this trip had been to bond with his son. Well, she snorted, that could be checked

FREE BOOKS GIVEAWAY

We pay for everything!

YOU pick your books – WE pay for everything.
You get up to FOUR New Books and TWO Mystery Gifts...absolutely FREE

Dear Reader,

I am writing to announce the launch of a huge **FREE BOOKS GIVEAWAY**... and to let you know that YOU are entitled to choose up to FOUR fantastic books that WE pay for.

Try **Harlequin® Desire** books featuring the worlds of the American elite with juicy plot twists, delicious sensuality and intriguing scandal.

Try **Harlequin Presents® Larger-Print** books featuring the glamourous lives of royals and billionaires in a world of exotic locations, where passion knows no bounds.

Or TRY BOTH!

In return, we ask just one favor: Would you please participate in our brief Reader Survey? We'd love to hear from you.

This FREE BOOKS GIVEAWAY means that we pay for *everything!* We'll even cover the shipping, and no purchase is necessary, now or later. So please return your survey today. You'll get **Two Free Books** and **Two Mystery Gifts** from each series to try, altogether worth over **$20!**

Sincerely

Pam Powers

Pam Powers
For Harlequin Reader Service

Complete the survey below and return it today to receive up to 4 FREE BOOKS and FREE GIFTS guaranteed!

FREE BOOKS GIVEAWAY
Reader Survey

1

Do you prefer stories with happy endings?

○ YES   ○ NO

2

Do you share your favorite books with friends?

○ YES   ○ NO

3

Do you often choose to read instead of watching TV?

○ YES   ○ NO

YES! Please send me my Free Rewards, consisting of **2 Free Books from each series I select** and **Free Mystery Gifts**. I understand that I am under no obligation to buy anything, as explained on the back of this card.

❏ Harlequin Desire® (225/326 HDL GQZ6)
❏ Harlequin Presents® Larger-Print (176/376 HDL GQZ6)
❏ Try Both (225/326 & 176/376 HDL GQ2J)

FIRST NAME

LAST NAME

ADDRESS

APT.#

CITY

STATE/PROV.

ZIP/POSTAL CODE

EMAIL ❏ Please check this box if you would like to receive newsletters and promotional emails from Harlequin Enterprises ULC and its affiliates. You can unsubscribe anytime.

HD/HP-520-FBG21

If offer card is missing write to: Harlequin Reader Service, P.O. Box 1341, Buffalo, NY 14240-8531 or visit www.ReaderService.com

BUSINESS REPLY MAIL

FIRST-CLASS MAIL   PERMIT NO. 717   BUFFALO, NY

POSTAGE WILL BE PAID BY ADDRESSEE

HARLEQUIN READER SERVICE

PO BOX 1341

BUFFALO NY 14240-8571

NO POSTAGE
NECESSARY
IF MAILED
IN THE
UNITED STATES

off the list. The other reason—hammering out the details of their arrangement—had yet to be accomplished.

God, she still couldn't believe she'd agreed to moving in with him. Before he'd arrived at her house, she'd been firmly entrenched on #TeamSeparateHouseholds. But Ross always had possessed a silver tongue—and a gifted one. No, dammit. Don't think of *that*.

But once that floodgate was opened, the waters rushed in, tugging her under.

That kiss. His mouth had brushed hers, and she'd gone up in lust-driven-pride-abandoning flames. Had he guessed from her reaction that she hadn't been with another man since him? That would be utterly humiliating. Especially as he'd been with countless women if the gossip magazines and sites were to be believed.

It hadn't been for lack of opportunity, but her priorities had been Ben and working. They'd left no time for dating or even casual hookups. Besides, the last time she'd trusted a man with her body, he'd let her down in the most spectacular of ways.

Obviously, her libido couldn't give a damn about that. Even now heat pooled and thickened, beading her nipples under her multiple layers and swelling the flesh between her legs. She shifted, her thighs sliding against each other, doing nothing to assuage the ache deep inside her. The man had always been able to turn her inside out with need. With him, she threw away every rule and expectation, stripped off every inhibition and became…his. His to use, to corrupt, to imprison in a world of pleasure that she never wanted to be free of.

His to cast aside when he was finished.

She sucked in a breath, the truth of that slamming into her like a solid punch.

Because he would do it. Just as he hadn't asked her to stay three years ago or come after her. Just as his arrangement already wore a predetermined expiration date.

Ross Edmond might be able to make her burn hotter than the sun, but he wasn't dependable. He wasn't a man for the long haul.

He wasn't *her* man.

"Mama!"

Her son's cry yanked her from her sobering thoughts, and when she lowered the cup to the railing and smiled, the warmth in the gesture was real despite the heaviness of her reality. Ben perched on Ross's shoulders, his chubby, short legs wrapped around his father's neck, his hands spread like little starfish on Ross's cheeks.

"Me!" Ben shouted, which she interpreted as "Look at me!" He patted Ross's face, ordering, "Daddy, go!"

Ross smiled, and cupping Ben's arms, he started slowly spinning around. The way their son screamed in glee, he might as well as have been on a roller coaster. Charlotte laughed at Ben's antics, but the warm joy lighting Ross's face? She pressed her hands to her chest and exhaled a long, shaky breath. Telling Ben that Ross was his "daddy" had been a spontaneous decision for her this morning. And in the face of Ross's happiness at being claimed—and ordered around—by his son, she could set any doubts aside that she'd made the right decision.

On that, at least.

"Are you hungry?" Ross called up to her.

When Ben yelled, "Eat!" in reply, his grin widened and softened at once.

"Ben cast his vote. How about you?"

"I could eat." She picked up her cup and jerked a thumb over her shoulder. "Let me go see what's in the refrigerator, and I can cook us something."

"No need." Ross tumbled Ben down into his arms, earning another delighted squeal of approval from their son. "This is supposed to be a rest for you, too. I already had dishes prepared. I got it."

And he certainly did.

A half hour later, she sat at the huge marble island in the middle of a kitchen that made her chef's soul weep with its top-of-the-line appliances. But could she expect less from a place with five bedrooms and bathrooms, a media room, a library, enough windows that a person could enjoy stellar views from each room and an elevator? An *elevator*, for God's sake. She shook her head.

"What?" Ross glanced at her over his shoulder, a glass baking dish in one hand and the other curled around the open stove door. "I think I can handle warming up a precooked meal," he drawled, eyebrow arched high.

She held up her hands, palms out. "I didn't say a word about your culinary skills," she swore. "Actually, I was thinking, how many TVs are needed in a place like this? I get having the theater-sized one in the living room and in the bedrooms. But there's one out by the hot tub *and* in each bathroom. The. Bathroom."

He snorted. "That you even have to ask that question has me questioning your reasoning. Seriously, Charlotte. What happens when nature calls and the Rangers are playing the Mariners? Am I supposed to just miss out on an important play? I think not."

"No." She smirked. "You just pause the game on one of your fifty DVRs and go like a big boy."

Ross chuckled. "Touché." He slid the dish in the oven and closed the door. "Ben is having a good time," he murmured, his gaze shifting to the toddler, who sat in front of the huge, dark brown sectional couch. Ben babbled to himself as he happily played with the mountain of toys that'd been waiting for him when they arrived at the cabin.

"How could he not?" she drawled. "It's like Christmas came early."

A corner of Ross's mouth kicked up as he shrugged a shoulder. "I might've gone a little overboard." At her snort, he held up his hands. "Fine. A *lot* overboard. But I have birthdays, Christmases and all the other gift-giving holidays to make up for." He paused and cocked his head to the side, studying her. "Do your parents know that you two are here with me?"

She shook her head. "I told them I was going on a business trip and that my manager's husband was coming along to watch Ben and their kids."

He nodded but his face had settled into an inscrutable mask that betrayed none of his thoughts. "When do you plan on telling them the truth about me?"

"Soon." She laughed softly, but nothing about this situation was remotely humorous. "Especially since we're apparently moving in together. My parents and I… As I mentioned before, we're in the process of re-building our relationship. And I'm more than a little worried about how this news is going to affect it."

"Yes, you told me a little bit about what happened with them," Ross said, leaning a hip against the counter behind him, crossing his arms over his chest. She tried—and failed—not to notice how the muscles flexed underneath his long-sleeved white Henley. The man could make arm porn a multi-million-dollar industry. "From what I remember, you and your parents used to be close."

"That was before I embarrassed them by getting pregnant out of wedlock. They were incredibly disappointed and disagreed with me raising the baby as a single mother. And they were very vocal about it."

Vestiges of the hurt echoed in her chest even though she'd forgiven her parents long ago.

"Needless to say, our relationship was strained for a while. It started to heal when Ben was born. They fell in love with him at first sight." She glanced over at her son, love swelling so hard it brushed away those whispers from the past like a broom sweeping out dirt from dark corners. "But I still never told them who his father was—and they never asked." She huffed, shaking her head. "They're going to have some explaining to do with their friends, though. People assumed I got married and divorced while I was in California, and they didn't disabuse anyone of that assumption. When it becomes known that you're Ben's father and that we've never been married, they're going to be scrambling."

"Are you angry with them?"

She didn't immediately answer. *What are you doing?* a small inner voice yelled at her. The last time she'd allowed herself to confide in this man, to trust in him, she'd set herself up for a heartbreak that had nearly broken her. Letting him in again would be a foolish mistake, and she'd promised herself long ago that she'd never be a fool for any man again. Particularly *this* man.

Yet… In a short time, they would be living together again. Co-parenting. They needed to have some sort of cordial relationship—some level of trust—to ensure Ben flourished in a healthy, calm environment. And that required her opening the door to Ross, even if only a little.

Sighing, she dipped her chin. "I was. They emotionally abandoned me just because I did something they didn't approve of. And I can't lie, there are moments when I still have a hard time wrapping my brain around the fact that I've forgiven them. But for the most part, I've let the anger go."

"For Ben's sake, are you going to be able to do the same with me?"

Her breath caught in her lungs, and she stared at him. At the electrifying blue eyes that smoldered with an intensity that simultaneously stirred the embers of desire inside her and set her veins racing with an inexplicable fear.

Discovering he hadn't known about her pregnancy and hadn't callously tossed her aside had gone a long way toward soothing her anger and resentment toward him. But a part of her clutched at the slick shards of bitterness that were embedded in her soul. Because that part hadn't forgiven him for not loving her, not needing her, for letting her go when all she'd wanted was to be his.

Before she could answer, Ben raced from the living room and up to her. He wrapped his arms around her legs and tipped his head back. "Mama, potty!" he announced.

Relief poured through her. Lord, she'd never been so happy to potty train her son. "Let's go," she said, grasping his chubby little hand in hers.

Ross's gaze seared her as she escaped his question and presence. A temporary reprieve. But one she was grateful for.

She needed the time to shore up her defenses against the force that was Ross Edmond.

"Is he finally down?" Charlotte glanced up from her glass of wine to smirk at Ross. He'd left the living room earlier to put Ben to bed.

A half hour ago.

"Yes." He sprawled at the end of the couch she sat curled up on, his long, muscled legs spread out before her. "Just out of curiosity—" he rolled his head toward her, eyes narrowed "—do you usually read three books to him before he goes to sleep?"

She snickered into her wine. "Not. Even. Close."

A grin flirted with his mouth. "I had a feeling I was being suckered. That kid's lucky he's so adorable."

"Here." She leaned forward and picked up the second wineglass on the coffee table in front of her. Offering it to Ross, she chuckled. "I thought you might need this when you eventually came out."

"I appreciate it." He accepted the glass, sipping the Moscato.

Her belly dipped at the sight of those firm but soft lips pressed to the rim and the up-and-down glide of the Adam's apple in his strong throat. Damn. She couldn't even look at Ross drink without getting hot. She needed an intervention. And more wine. Grabbing the bottle off the table, she topped off her drink.

"Maybe we should talk over how we're going to make the living arrangements work," she suggested, desperate to concentrate on anything other than Ross, his lush mouth and his sexy throat muscles.

"Right," he agreed, taking another sip. "When we return, we can start looking for a house. But until we find one—" he set the wineglass on an end table "—staying at the ranch makes the most sense."

"I said no," Charlotte said, her answer automatic and adamant. "I'm not staying there, Ross. I thought we were through discussing that."

"I'm trying to understand why you're so against it. Is it because you used to work there, and that makes you uncomfortable? Or is it because it's where you and I—"

"No," she interrupted, not wanting him to finish that sentence. Not wanting to hear him describe what they used to do. Meet up? Fuck? Make love? "Like I said before, I've been independent for a long time. And you know how your father operates, Ross. He will try to run our lives if we're under his roof."

It was as close to the truth as she could come.

How could she explain to him that she dreaded being back under Rusty's thumb? Because if Rusty chose to pick up where he'd left off flirting with her, hitting on her, then he wouldn't find the same vulnerable girl; she wouldn't run scared. He would force her hand in telling Ross the real reason she'd been so eager to leave his father's employ. That Rusty couldn't keep his inappropriate comments to himself, and she feared that one day he wouldn't let it go at just talk. From the few times Ross had confided in her—and from her own two eyes—she could tell father and son didn't share a close, affectionate relationship. But Ross wanted more from his father…yearned for more. She refused to be responsible for torpedoing whatever chances they had of achieving that.

But deep inside her resided another reason. A reason that walked hand-in-hand with her insecurities. Just as she hadn't trusted Ross three years ago to have her back with his father, to stand up to him, she couldn't say with certainty that he would today, if he had to choose between Rusty and her and Ben. Rusty was a powerful, charismatic and domineering force. And for a son who looked up to his father, hungered for his acceptance and love… Ross might want to have her and Ben in his life, but if it came down to it, would he fight for them?

She didn't know.

And didn't want to find out.

Therefore, living at Elegance Ranch remained out of the question.

"I need you to just accept my decision."

Ross studied her, and she silently ordered herself not to flinch, not to betray any reaction to that blue, piercing stare. "Fine," he murmured. "But I am asking one thing."

She dipped her chin, indicating for him to continue.

"When we return back to Royal, come with me to introduce Ben to my family. We don't have to stay at the ranch, but I would like you there."

Though a barb-tipped unease clung to her ribs like

burrs, she nodded again. "Okay," she conceded. "I can do that."

Even if she'd rather eat a plate of boiled okra first. With hot sauce.

But if he met her halfway with not forcing the issue of the ranch, then she could do this. As long as she didn't have to spend too much time in Rusty's company.

"What is your work schedule like?" he asked, picking up his glass again.

"Monday through Saturday. I go in at about twelve thirty to help with food prep and then I don't leave until after closing. It's long hours, but it's also why I insisted on Sundays off so I could spend a whole day with Ben. I was taking a chance including that demand in my contract, since most chefs work seven days a week, including holidays. But Jeremy agreed, and I have a wonderful sous-chef as well as an excellent staff to cover me."

"Those are long hours," he murmured. "How did you juggle the job and a new baby in California?"

"Let's just say I haven't slept a full night for over two years," she replied dryly. "But I leaned a lot from my sister and her family. They were invaluable. Now I have a babysitter for Ben, and my parents take him often, as well."

"I have another proposition for you to consider. Let me take Ben while you're at work." He shifted toward her, forestalling her instinctive objection. "My schedule is more flexible than yours. When you leave for work, you can drop him off to me. The office has a day care for all of our employees. So I can visit him throughout the day. And after I leave, we can come over to the restaurant and have dinner with you on your break."

She blinked, stunned into silence.

How many times had she wished that her parents would offer to bring Ben by her job so she could see him? Being a single mother with a very demanding job, she constantly battled the guilt of not being there enough for her son. Of missing out on so many little things—like his giggle at a TV show or cuddling with him at bedtime. Building her career wasn't just for her success or fame; it was for Ben, too. She not only desired to provide for him, but to show him that no dream, no goal was too far or big for him to achieve. Even more than being a master chef, she hoped to be her child's inspiration.

But being his inspiration sometimes cost her time with him. *Precious* time.

"I—" She cleared her throat. "If you're sure it wouldn't be an inconvenience..."

"My son could never be an inconvenience."

His son. Not her.

Good. She was glad he said that. It served as a reminder that their sole connection was the child they had together.

"Thank you, then." She wrapped both hands around the bowl of her wineglass. "We can do that." Lowering her gaze, she studied the ruby depths as if it were a scrying glass. "I'm afraid to trust in this," she whispered, the confession slipping from her without her conscious permission.

"In this...or in me?"

She jerked her gaze up, meeting his shuttered scrutiny. *Retreat*, a voice hissed. *Retreat into casual chit-*

chat and surface topics. Because those subjects didn't tread on ground she'd burned long ago.

"Both." *Dammit*.

"I asked you before, but you didn't answer." He swirled the wine in his glass, but his unwavering stare remained on her. "You let your anger go with your parents, for Ben's sake. Have you done the same with me?"

"Have *you*?" she shot back, yes, avoiding that question. It was too loaded…too dangerous. Pitted with minefields she dreaded maneuvering.

Several seconds ticked by where only the crackle of logs burning in the cavernous fireplace filled the space. She waited with bated breath, every part of her clamoring for his reply.

"Yes," he said. "Knowing the circumstances and knowing you didn't intentionally keep me from Ben, I'm not angry anymore."

"Liar." Good Lord, her mouth had launched a rebellion, and she couldn't bring it back under control.

Ross arched an eyebrow. Didn't speak. But his eyes… No longer shadowed, they gleamed with—what? Surprise? Anger? Something darker…hunger?

"A part of you will always blame me for missing the first couple of years with Ben. But that's not even what you're lying about."

"Really? Enlighten me then, Charlotte."

"You still haven't forgiven me for leaving in the first place," she said brazenly. "Before you knew about Ben, you seethed with that anger, Ross. And it didn't just disappear."

Deliberately, Ross set the glass down on the end table. He stretched an arm out along the back of the couch, and the other settled on his thick thigh, long fingers splayed wide. But he didn't look at her, his attention seemingly transfixed on the fireplace's dancing orange-and-red flames.

"You think you know me? That's presumptuous of you, isn't it?" he murmured, no rancor in his low voice, but she caught the edge. Sharp enough to leave stinging cuts.

"I knew you better than most," she said, and at her words his head turned toward her, and the icy shock of his wintry blue gaze slicked over her skin like sleet.

"We fucked, Charlotte," he stated bluntly.

Though he spoke the truth, it still drove a fist into her stomach, leaving her winded and hurting. Because he said what she'd always known but had mourned. For him, it had been just sex with the family chef. For her, it had been so much more. And that was her fault, not his. But wisdom didn't mean shit when the heart became involved. Lucky for her, she'd stopped being that foolish, naive girl three years earlier.

"And yet, you still resent me. Come on, Ross, get it off your chest now that you have the chance. Want to tell me why?" She taunted him, and fire leaped in his eyes as if she'd poked those flames.

Did she want to be burned?

Yes.

The word vaulted, unbidden, to her mind. And she wanted to deny that need, but her actions belied it.

"What are you doing?" His hooded scrutiny dipped to her mouth, then lower. Over her suddenly sensitive breasts, down to her thighs…to the aching space between them. When his gaze met hers again, the heat from it licked at her skin.

God, she wanted to lean into it. Bask in its warmth. Let it consume her.

Even though every self-preserving instinct screamed at her to protect herself.

"I don't know what you mean," she said, the rasp of the tone making a mockery of the statement.

His sensual lips curved at one corner, lending it a carnal, almost cruel cast. "Don't you? Do you want a fight, baby? Is that it?" he murmured. "Or do you just want to use it as an excuse to get your mouth on me?" He cocked his head, and his teeth briefly sank into his bottom lip as if he were nipping her mouth instead of his own. "You don't need that charade, Charlotte. If you want to taste me without having to feel guilty afterward, it can be our little secret."

Little secret. The words clanged in her head, a warning bell.

That's all you are to him. All you've ever been.

Truth. She *knew this*. Yet…lust pumped through her like an engine with greased, faulty brakes—fast, screaming, out of control.

Maybe he was right; she did want his anger to take the decision out of her hands so she could give in. So she could blame emotion instead of accepting that she wanted his mouth again. Craved his tongue licking at her, sucking on her.

A kiss. That was all she'd allow herself. Another kiss. Then she could sate this need that had been teasing and taunting her since yesterday. For three years, she'd been sacrificing—for her career, for her son.

Tonight, she could take for herself. Just once.

One little taste. Who could it hurt?

You.

Bullshit. Because she wouldn't let it.

"That's nothing new for us, is it?" she whispered. Rising from the couch, she slowly moved across the short distance separating them. "Secrets. We're made of them. So what's one more, right?" She pressed a knee into the cushion along his outer thigh. "Except this time, you're mine. I'm not yours."

"Charlotte." A faint frown marred his brow as she lifted her other leg, straddling him, caging him between her thighs. His hands shot up to cradle her hips. "What're you—"

"Taking."

Without breaking his gaze, she lifted her glass, sipped. Then, turning it around so his lips would close over the same spot, offered it to him. He accepted the drink, and the intimacy of the gesture had her sex clenching, an empty ache pulsing deep inside her.

The moment he lifted his head, she dipped a fingertip in the wine, swirling it. Setting the glass on the end table next to his, she turned back to him and slowly, sensually painted first his top and then the fuller bottom one with the wine. She stared at his stained mouth, her breath a ragged, heated thing in her chest.

Lowering her head, she hovered above him, halfway expecting him to tilt his head back and confiscate this kiss. But with his blue eyes like crystal flames in a face of harsh, almost severe angles, he didn't move. Just watched her. Waited. And for a man accustomed to control in the bedroom and out, this show of temporary submission was unusual…and hot as hell.

A moan caressed her throat, but she trapped it, not willing to betray the erotic storm that whipped and howled through her body. And she hadn't even kissed him yet. But she'd rectify that.

Now.

Curling her fingers around the back of the couch, she closed the scant distance between them. Swept her tongue over his plush bottom lip. Tasted Moscato and him. Again, she locked down that telltale moan. She repeated the stroke over his top lip, drawing the flesh between her teeth, sucking every bit of the wine from him.

His grip on her hips tightened, his fingers digging into her skin. What did it say about her that she secretly hoped he would mark her, leave a souvenir from this taboo and unwise pocket of time? Either that she was desperate or sad, or a total sucker for this man's possession.

Probably all three.

Shoving the distressing thought aside, she sank into the kiss, stroking her tongue between his lips, tangling with him, sliding against him, licking at him. That raw sandalwood, rain and Texas wind scent that clung to his skin was stronger here inside his mouth. Richer. Even more delicious. She could drown in his taste. Drown in this almost overwhelming sensation of heat, liquid lust and pleasure.

The moan she'd been so determined to rein in broke free, and she released the sound into his mouth. His tongue curled around it, claimed it as his own, and with a tilt of his head and a hard thrust, demanded another.

And God help her, but she gave it to him. Surrendered it, along with the control she'd wielded but now wanted him to seize.

As if sensing the shift, he grabbed her ponytail, tugged hard on it, jerking her head back. Smoking lightning bolts of need struck her, and the whimper that escaped her would probably bring the sting of humiliation later, but not right now. Now she closed her eyes, relishing the sting across her scalp, dwelling in the sense of vulnerability from her exposed throat.

"If you're going to be sorry for this later," Ross murmured against her skin, his breath a hot, damp caress, "then I'm going to give you something to really regret."

Then he dragged his teeth down her neck, the slight burn vibrating through her so it reverberated in her nipples, down her spine, in her sex. And when he clamped a firm, possessive bite on the crook where her neck and shoulder met...

"Ross," she groaned, loosening her clutch on the couch to burrow her fingers through his thick, dark blond hair, fisting it. Holding him to her.

"Missed that," he growled, rubbing his lips over the spot that had just received his teeth. "Missed the sound of my name when I'm about to give you what you need. And you need this, don't you, baby?"

She shuddered, her grasp on him tightening. The scraps of reason that still remained forbade her to answer, to give him this ammunition against her. But those remnants didn't stand a chance against the lust coursing swollen and unchecked through her body.

"Yes," she gasped. "Give it to me."

His dark chuckle tickled her skin, a faintly menacing warning wrapped in seductive, rough silk. "Ask for it. Nicely."

For real? She ground her teeth together, trapping the order to "get on with it." Because past experience had taught her that when he was in this kind of mood, a taunting mood where anger roiled just below the hunger, he could—would—drag out this pleasurable torture until she begged for what only he could deliver. An ecstasy that would break her.

"Ross, I need—" The word *you* lodged in her throat. But she didn't need *him*; she needed what he did to her body. Two different things as he'd so expertly shown her. "I need you to make me come."

"Damn right you do," he rasped, and hauling her head down, he crushed his mouth to hers.

This kiss was fire and ice. Gasoline and cooling water.

A reunion and searing loss.

He ate at her lips, and she tilted her head, serving herself up. Leaving her mouth tender and wet, he dragged stinging kisses down her chin, lower to her neck and lower still to her collarbone. He paused, sucking the thin skin there between his lips, marking her. And she loved it. Silently urged him to suck harder, *longer*.

Impatient fingers gripped the bottom of her sweater and yanked it up and over her head. For a moment, panic flared bright inside her, and she almost lifted her hand to her neck. But then, she barely managed not going limp in relief. She'd removed the necklace and pendant before leaving the house. *Thank God*. What would his reaction be if he saw she'd kept it? She shook her head as if that could erase even the possibility.

"What's wrong? Where'd you go?" he murmured, tossing her top to the couch, leaving her clad in only a thin tank top and a black, scalloped lace bra. Being a chef who worked long hours, most of the time her body only knew chef coats, T-shirts and black pants. As a concession to the woman who loved fashion, she had an addiction for pretty underwear. And the desire flaring in those light eyes telegraphed his approval.

"Nothing," she replied, skimming her fingers over his shoulders and avoiding his gaze. "Nowhere."

He didn't call her on her bullshit; instead he slowly slid a hand up her side, rucking the tank top so the fire-warmed air brushed her exposed skin. She held her breath, her chest lifting and falling on her deep, labored breaths. Oh, God. It'd been so long. And she ached so much. *Touch me.* The words screamed in her head like a pissed-off banshee. *I need. I need. I need.*

The chant exploded in her head like pop rockets, quick, loud and bright.

His lips closed over her nipple. And she cried out. Jerked in his hold. Melted against him.

"Shh," he soothed, sweeping his lips over the tip through her thin top and bra.

They proved to be an insubstantial barrier to his tongue, his teeth, his passion. He drew on her, alternating with a quick lash and a lush lick. Big, capable hands cupped her, molded her, lifted her to his lips and plucked at the peak that hadn't received his mouth yet.

She sank onto his lap, her sex grinding against the steely length of his cock. With a ragged groan, she tipped her head back on her shoulders, clinging to his head and working his erection. Lust had a way of burning away good sense, shame and inhibition. And as she rode him, circling her hips, bucking against him, racing toward an ending that she would gladly fly into, she shed all of them.

With an impatient growl, Ross tugged down the top of her tank and her bra cup. That needy sound roughened as he bared her to his gaze and his mouth. He switched to her neglected breast, drawing it deep to grant it the same erotic attention, and she trembled, unable to tear her enraptured gaze from the sight of him loving her body. His hand slipped down her belly, not stopping at the waistband of her black leggings, but sliding underneath. Drifting lower... Until he stroked a caress over wet, aching flesh.

"Ross," she breathed, stiffening as pleasure arced through her, momentarily stunning her. His attention on her breasts—God, yes, it was good. But this? This light but firm strumming of the taut nerves cresting her sex? The delicious stroke between her swollen folds? This defied "good" and rammed straight into "exquisite."

"I need it," she pleaded, hips jerking and rolling in an uncontrolled rhythm. "I need it so badly. Please."

Hunger reduced pride to smoldering cinders. Desperation razed caution to the ground. She wanted this man with a desire that should've scared her. Maybe later, when lust didn't cloud her mind, it would. But not at this moment, with those elegant fingers swirling a diabolical caress around that sensitive nub. Not when she hovered on the verge of coming apart with him for the first time in three long years.

He hushed her, freeing her breast with a soft pop then reclaiming her mouth again. The indulgent thrust of his tongue, the luxurious tangle reflected his touch down below. He glided through her sex, fingers flirting with her entrance before slowly, deliberately pumping into her.

She cried into his mouth, and he greedily took it. On a rumble of pleasure, of approval, he withdrew, then stroked back into her, burying one then two fingers inside her grasping core. Pleasure spun, a crazy, blinding storm that built and built, threatening to sweep her away and never return her to who she'd been before she made the impulsive decision to start this.

Her fingers scrabbled at his shoulders, clutching at his head, as she held on for the inevitable climax. Yet, even as her hips bucked and ground against his hand, her body demanding more, she fought that ending. She feared never feeling this again, never *having* this again.

Pushing the thought aside, she buried her face in his throat and chanted soundless words against his skin. But maybe he heard them, because he thrust harder. Curled his fingertips against that high, soft-and-hard place so deep inside her.

And she surrendered.

To the pleasure. To the power. To the lust.

She shattered, and as his low, insistent and ragged voice urged her to fuck his fingers, to take everything, she threw herself into the fire, knowing she would emerge scarred, marked…

Changed.

And not for the better.

Nine

"Thank you for leaving work early to do this with me." Ross glanced across the middle console of his Aston Martin toward the silent woman perched on the passenger seat.

Charlotte stared out the window, her hands folded on top of her thighs, her spine poker straight. His gaze trailed over the tight bun of her hair, the almost fragile beauty of her profile and the sensual pout of her mouth. Clenching his jaw, he dragged his perusal back to the road where it belonged. Where it was safer for a number of reasons.

Aside from the obvious, with his attention focused squarely on driving, he couldn't stare at her and reminisce on how good that mouth had softened against his. How the flavor of her still lingered nearly two days later. How he could still feel the tight grip and flutter of her silken, hot sex on his fingers.

Jesus, she'd nearly burned him alive. The memories of how they'd been together hadn't compared to the reality of Charlotte in his arms, twisting on his lap, screaming in release. A shiver rippled through him, and he shifted on his seat, his body stirring, hardening. This was what she did to him. And it scared him what he'd do—what he'd give up—just for another chance to have her over him. Under him.

To be inside her.

"I agreed to go to the ranch with you and introduce Ben to your family," she murmured, yanking him from his thoughts. Thankful for the distraction, Ross checked the rearview mirror to see their son asleep in his car seat.

It was nine o'clock at night, which was past his bedtime. But when they returned from Telluride the day before, Rusty hadn't been in town. He'd just arrived this afternoon, and Ross didn't want to put this introduction off any longer. His father, Gina and Asher needed to meet his son, so they could all start on this road to being family. He didn't worry about his sister and brother as much as Rusty. But Ross clung to the hope that once his father laid eyes on this beautiful little boy, he would set aside his stubbornness and anger and embrace him as his grandson. Embrace Ben's mother, as well.

"Does Rusty know that we're coming?" she asked in that same even, flat tone that contained no emotion.

He tossed another glance in her direction. That note in her voice. It rubbed him the wrong way. As did her reluctance to even *visit* the ranch. He accepted her reasons for not wanting to live at his home, even if he still didn't agree with them. But something small, almost undecipherable continued to needle him like an irritating bee sting. Like there was more to her objection than she was telling him...

"Ross?"

He gave his head an abrupt shake. "Yes," he replied, his fingers curling around the steering wheel in a tighter grip. "I spoke with him earlier and told him we were coming over. And why."

"I hope this turns out the way you want," she said. "For your sake, I really do."

He didn't reply because the turnoff to Elegance Ranch appeared before him. Yet, it didn't prevent an ominous trickle from tripping down his spine. Shaking it off, he slowly drove to the big gate with its elegant scrolls of *E* and *R* worked into the black iron, and lowered his visor. He and Rusty had experienced their difficulties and disagreements, but when it came down to it, family and the Edmond name meant more to his father than anything else. Rusty might threaten, but he'd never abandoned him like Ross's mother had. Grim assurance rolled through him as he pressed the button on the automatic gate opener. No, Rusty was guilty of a lot of things but he wouldn't—

"Son of a bitch," he growled. He jabbed the button again. But the gate remained shut. "He did it," he whispered, shock crackling through him on an electrified, discordant wave. "The bastard really did it."

Grief and anger crashed fast on the heels of the astonishment. Hadn't he just thought his father, who claimed family to be more important than everything, wouldn't cut him loose? Had Gina and Asher known what he'd planned? Would they abandon him, too?

A yawning vacuum opened inside his chest. *Alone.* He was alone, and the emptiness threatened to swallow him whole. In an instant of time, he was swept back to that ten year-old boy who watched his mother walk out of their house. This void had swamped him then, too, and he'd tried to fill it with the stingy love and approval of the only consistent parent he'd had left. And now he didn't even have that.

He'd been rejected, discarded.

Again.

"Ross, what's wrong?" A hand settled on his taut forearm, and only then did he realize that he had such a stranglehold on the steering wheel that his knuckles had blanched white. Peeling his hand free, he flexed the fingers, the blood rushing back into them with a tingle. He turned to Charlotte, who studied him in the deepening darkness, with a slight frown.

"I can't open the gate," he murmured, still staring at it as if at any moment it would belatedly swing open. He laughed, and the bitterness of it filled the interior. "He essentially changed the locks on me so I can't enter the property. My father kicked me out." Out of the house. Out of the family.

"Damn," she whispered. Her fingers curled around his arm, squeezing gently. "I'm sorry, Ross. I'm—"

"Doesn't matter," he cut her off, shifting the gear into Reverse and then hooking his arm over the back of her seat so he could turn the car around. At the same time, shaking off her touch. He couldn't handle her sympathy—her pity—right now.

Not when the betrayal, the fucking hurt, of the person who was supposed to love him, support him, *accept* him, tore at him with greedy, poisonous claws. The temptation to pull over, call Rusty and try to convince him to reconsider tugged at Ross. Hard. But Rusty had not only passed down his name to him. He'd bequeathed to Ross his stubbornness, as well. And Ross refused to beg his father for anything. Especially to let him come home.

He hadn't run after his mother.

He hadn't run after Charlotte.

Damned if he would with his father, either.

"Ross," Charlotte said, and her soft voice with its hint of worry scraped over his senses, leaving emotional welts.

"Sorry about needlessly taking you away from work. I'll drop you two back off at your house," he interrupted her again.

"Where will you go?"

He shrugged a shoulder, the gesture deliberately nonchalant. "I'll grab a hotel room for now. Doesn't matter." Goddamn, he was getting tired of saying those two words. Of *needing* to say them. "We planned on looking for a house together anyway."

Silence hummed in the car for several moments, and he could feel the weight of her speculation.

"We're going with you."

He whipped his head to the side, spearing her with a quick glance before returning his attention to the road. But that look had been enough to glimpse the resolve in her expression.

"No, that's not necessary," he said with a shake of his head.

"Maybe not, but we're still doing it."

"Charlotte—" he snapped.

"I'm not leaving you alone tonight," she murmured. "You were just cut off from your family several minutes ago. I know what that's like. To feel alone. Without the anchor you always counted on to be there." Her voice trailed off. But a second later, she cleared her throat. "So no, Ben and I are going with you. And tomorrow morning, we start the house search."

"I don't need your pity," he ground out.

Another beat of silence. "How about my friendship?"

The objection welled in his throat again and pushed onto his tongue. But that part of him…the part of him that constantly surrounded himself with people, parties, with *noise* because he hated the deafening and crushing silence of loneliness, smothered the prideful rejection.

"Okay."

Ross paced the sunken living room of the luxurious hotel suite, his fingers clasping the tumbler of scotch ferociously tight. Either as a desperate lifeline or a potential weapon, he couldn't decide at the moment. Maybe after several more sips, he could weigh in more decisively.

Thrusting his other hand through his hair, he stalked to the floor-to-ceiling glass wall and stared out over the lavish gardens that The Bellamy, Royal's five-star resort, boasted. Usually, when he had occasion to visit The Silver Saddle bar or enjoy fine farm-to-table dining at The Glass House, both housed within the luxury hotel, he paused to appreciate its beauty. Inspired by George Vanderbilt's iconic French Renaissance chateau in North Carolina, Deacon Price and Shane Delgado had built its newer, hipper cousin. With over fifty acres of gorgeous gardens, a spa, two hundred and fifty richly appointed en suites that included the latest in technology and amenities, The Bellamy was a crown jewel in Royal.

And for the first time since stepping foot in the resort, his corporate credit card had been declined.

He downed another swallow of alcohol, the burn of it mingling with the fury that still seethed in his chest. Not only had his father banned him from the only home he'd ever known, but he'd cut him off financially. Trying to break him. To make him heel like a naughty puppy.

But he wasn't anyone's pet.

And he had resources and investments his father couldn't touch. He'd use those to purchase a home for him, his son and Charlotte.

And he also had the name Rusty had given him. Ross had used *that* to place this stay on his own tab.

Turned out the one thing that was so important to Rusty, he couldn't snatch away from Ross. He smirked down into the drink. The irony didn't escape him.

"Ben is asleep." Charlotte's voice reached him, wrapping around his chest, sinking into him. With his back to her, he briefly closed his eyes, savoring that low, husky tone. "Considering it's late, he didn't put up much of a fight." A small hand settled just below his shoulder blade. "Ross, are you okay?"

"I'm fine," he replied, not removing his stare from the amber alcohol.

She released an impatient sound that landed somewhere between a scoff and a tsk. "You're *not* fine. How could you be?" She moved in front of him, and he lifted his head, meeting the concern in her brown eyes. "Listen, I know we're feeling our way through being co-parents and possibly friends, but you can talk to me. Like you used to."

"That's when we were naked and sex had loosened my mouth," he drawled. Yes, he was being an asshole. But agreeing to her staying with him had been a bad decision. He was too on edge. Too angry. Too raw. And with her scent teasing his nose, her beautiful eyes on him and that gorgeous body close, he was too reckless.

She had every right to snap at him for his crass reply. Instead, she silently studied him. And like a coward, he turned away, striding back over to the bar to refresh his drink. And avoid that piercing scrutiny.

"Now who's spoiling for a fight?" she murmured, lobbing a variation of his words from the cabin back at him. "Classic Ross Edmond move," she taunted.

Bile churned in his gut, but he shoved it back down, nursing the bitterness. Anger was better than the emasculating need to curl his arms around her and lean on her, until not every breath he took carried the ache of loneliness. "Lash out. Hurt before they can hurt you. Push away so no one can see that you actually feel. You told me it was presumptuous of me to claim I knew you. But some things haven't changed in three years."

He didn't see her approach him again, but the thick, cream carpet couldn't muffle her footsteps. And the hand that, once more, rested on his shoulder blade seemed to singe him through his shirt, branding him.

His movements turned jerky, and a little of the scotch spilled over the rim of the glass as he splashed the alcohol into the tumbler. Quickly recapping the decanter and smacking it back down on the bar, he seized the drink and downed a big swallow.

Only then did he step away from her—from her and the hand that he didn't want on his back. No, he wanted those delicate, skillful fingers farther south. Wrapped around him. Squeezing him and trading one pain for another.

"I don't want to fight, Charlotte. But I'm beginning to suspect maybe there's another reason you're out here pushing me. Maybe there's something you want from me other than…honesty," he said, sipping slower as he faced her. Making a show of scanning her from head to toe, his eyes drifted down the blue-and-white ruffled shirt and slim navy pants she'd changed into for the meeting with his family and to the tips of her black stilettos.

On the deliberate path back up all those delicious curves and dips, he struggled not to reveal how she affected him. Had him damn near trembling inside with the flare of heat and a need that burrowed deeper than simple lust. Fuck, what was he doing? What danger was he courting? In his current state, she was kindling thrown on an already simmering fire. It wouldn't require much for the flames to rage higher, hotter and out of control.

"You used to do that, too," she said, tilting her head to the side. If his words or perusal had offended her, she did an admirable job of concealing it.

"Do what?" he asked, interjecting a boredom into

his voice that he hoped covered the razor-thin shards of panic cutting into him.

"Use sex to avoid a conversation."

"Oh, baby, if I were using sex you would know it." He rubbed his thumb over his bottom lip, smothering a groan as her gaze tracked the motion with a fascination that she would undoubtedly hate him for noticing. "Did you forget so easily? Do you need a refresher course? First, there wouldn't be a need for conversation. Not with that greedy little tongue of yours seeking mine out, tangling with me. Getting wild with me. The second hint would be those pretty but inconvenient clothes sliding off, revealing that dick tease of a body. Third would be the needy sound you make at the back of your throat when I kiss the tops of your breasts, suck on those hard nipples or cup that beautiful ass. Fourth would be the shiver that never fails to telegraph how close you are to coming. All it would take is a touch, a stroke over that tight, wet—"

"Stop," she rasped.

It should've been triumph that crackled through him as his gaze dropped to the rapid rise and fall of her chest. But the dark thing with claws tearing at him wasn't victory.

It was lust.

Hunger.

His plan to shut her up, to drive her away, had backfired.

Big-time.

"That's not a word you would be uttering," he rumbled, mimicking her previous action and cocking his head. "Not unless 'don't' preceded it. Don't stop. More.

Harder," he recited. "That's the only conversation we'd have."

"Ross, you think I can't see you're upset? That you're hurting?" she stubbornly continued, even though those expressive brown eyes gleamed, and the tight points of her nipples jutted against her shirt.

"I never claimed I wasn't hurting," he drawled, setting the glass on the bar. He then shifted forward so close she tipped her head back to maintain eye contact. "Let me show you where."

He grasped her wrist and drew her hand forward, slowly enough that she had more than enough time to glean his intention. And that same amount of time to yank her arm back. But she didn't stop him as he pressed her palm to his cock. Didn't hiss an objection when he instinctively ground against it.

No, it was his curse that assaulted the air, his hand that threw hers off.

He who wheeled around and stalked across the room.

"Go to bed, Charlotte," he ordered, voice shredded, control not too far behind. "It's been a long day for both of us."

He needed her gone, preferably tucked away behind a locked door. With the imprint of her palm branded on his dick, he couldn't guarantee he could keep his hands off her. And nothing good would come of that. Not with desire and anger roiling inside him, urging him to wreck the tentative truce they'd forged with hot, filthy sex. Because there would be nothing cleansing about what he'd do to her. *Take her. Conquer her. Corrupt her.* That was the kind of fucking he'd indulge in and demand from her to sublimate this rage, this pain.

"Not until you talk to me."

He snarled, sharply pivoting and charging back across the room. *Calm. Keep your distance.* The judicious warnings whispered through his mind, but they were reduced to ash underneath the burning riot of emotions. He didn't stop when he approached her. Didn't halt until her back pressed against the window and his palms slapped on either side of her head, caging her between glass and his body.

"Why are you pushing this?" he growled, lowering his head until his lips grazed the curve of her ear. "What do you want to hear from me? That my father is a bastard? That he evicted me like some random tenant? That he cut me off, and I'm angry as hell? Yes, dammit. Are you happy? I'm shocked, furious and even a little scared. All of that. But he isn't the first person to walk away from me, Charlotte. I'm a fucking pro at this. So save the sympathy, the pity. I don't need them. What I *do* need is for you to take your sweet ass into that bedroom, lie down next to our son and leave me alone. For both our sakes."

He shoved off the window, air plowing out of his lungs. Dammit. He hadn't meant to say any of that. But her nearness, this unrelenting need and his hurt had propelled the words off his tongue, and not even God could turn back time to erase the too-revealing confession. Slowly he backed away from her, his narrowed gaze fixed on her face. A face that betrayed her surprise and, heaven help him, resolve.

He walked away. Again. Hell, if she wouldn't leave, he would. His pride had disintegrated and littered the floor around his feet. What was one more retreat?

Her hand circled his wrist.

And the last, tattered scraps of his control crumbled.

Turning, he simultaneously lunged for her, cupping her face between his hands, tilting her head back. Her fingers curled into his shirt, holding on. Probably to maintain her balance, since he leaned over her so far that her back arched, her full breasts pressing to his chest.

He shuddered.

"Goddammit, Charlotte," he bit out, lips moving over hers. "Leave now or stay and let me use you to pound out this…thing inside me. I won't be gentle—I can't be. I'll take from you, and I can't promise to give anything back. I want to feast on you and not stop until we're too broken to even breathe." He crushed a hard kiss to her mouth, thrusting between her lips in a quick taste-and-tangle that did nothing to satisfy the craving for her. "This is your chance to walk away now, baby. Because I can't."

Harsh puffs of air bathed his lips as her fingers encircled his wrists. But not to haul them away from her face. This brave, beautiful and *foolish* woman rose on her toes and took the next kiss. Opened wide for him. Allowed him entrance. Invited him to devour.

And on a groan heavy with desire, with demand— with gratitude—he accepted.

From the onset, the kiss consumed. Raw. Carnal. Ravenous. He went wild at her taste, diving back for more, always for more. Each lick, each slide of tongues, each rub of lips and bite of teeth ratcheted the desire consuming him to combustible levels. What was it about her that could transform him into this insatiable animal that was ready to snarl, claw and maul to keep her for himself?

Tonight, the last shred of reason interjected. This was just about here and now. Getting through the night. The only "forever" between him and Charlotte was Ben.

On the tail end of that thought, Ross sidestepped, maneuvering her so she backpedaled toward the couch. Without breaking the mating of their mouths, he guided her down to the cushion. As soon as she sat, he pushed between her legs, cupping her knees and spreading her wider to accommodate his torso.

He broke off the kiss, leaned back and watched his hands stroke up her toned, sexy legs, his fingertips skirting the crease where her thigh and upper body met. Didn't matter that she still wore her clothes. Her warmth seeped past the material to his skin, and he swore her rich fig-and-sugar scent was deeper, denser… headier. His gaze shifted higher, focusing on the cloth-covered flesh between her legs, and he slicked the tip of his tongue over his bottom lip. The source of that scent, that flavor emanated from right there.

And he wanted to gorge on it.

"If you really care about this shirt, you need to take it off now. I won't be as careful with it," he advised, raising his gaze from her sex to her face.

Her lips, swollen and damp from his kiss, parted, and a soft gust of breath eased past them. He almost leaned forward to feel that puff of air on his mouth, but he didn't. Couldn't risk missing her unveil herself for him.

Silence pulsed in the room, a thunderous heartbeat that nearly drowned out his own as he studied those elegant fingers move to the hidden buttons behind the ruffle that stretched from her throat to her waist. Quickly, she undid her shirt and peeled the two sides apart, revealing another of those sexy-as-hell confections others would call a bra. Pale green this time. Silk and lace molded to her luscious breasts. His mouth watered for a taste. And he didn't wait for her to shrug completely free of it before bowing over her and sucking a nipple deep into his mouth.

With a hushed curse, she battled the cuffs of her shirt, and he took advantage of her bound hands, cupping one breast, pinching the tip, rolling it while tonguing the other. Her tortured whimper mingled with his groan, and then her fingernails were scraping across his scalp, and he was popping the bra's front closure and freeing her.

Jesus. She was too fucking beautiful for words.

Switching breasts, he nuzzled the other mound, licking a path toward the peak. She arched into him, urging him on with whispered chants of his name, pressing his head to her, lowering a hand and closing it over his, so they squeezed and caressed together.

"Damn, I can't get enough of you," he muttered, brushing his lips over her wet nipple, then trailing a path punctuated by stinging kisses down her softly rounded stomach, pausing to trace the faint stretch marks over her skin. Marks that gave testimony to the precious life she'd brought into this world.

"Ross," she breathed, her fingers massaging his scalp, tugging at his hair. Trying to get him to look at her.

But he refused, couldn't. To do that, to gaze into those chocolate eyes, might trick him into believing this wasn't just a physical release. No, he wanted to get lost in her body, in the pleasure, not silly, deceptive notions of *more*. He skimmed one more caress over the light lines on her stomach, then continued lower. And when his lips bumped the waistband of her pants, he didn't hesitate to pop the closure, unzip and tug them down and off her.

For a moment, he froze. Drinking her in. All that smooth, silken almond skin clad in only green lace. And then, with one yank, not even that.

"Baby," he growled, raking his teeth across her hip. She jerked, a low cry escaping her. "Easy," he soothed, sweeping his tongue across the same path. "Hold on to me."

He issued the command, palming her inner thighs and spreading her wider. On a dark, hungry snarl, he dove into her. He barely heard her sharp scream, almost didn't feel the bite of her nails in his shoulders. Everything in him focused on her concentrated scent, the addictive taste and her slick flesh. God, he tried to slow down, to invoke the control he was known for. But that proved impossible. With each lap, suckle and swirl of his tongue and lips, he lost more of himself. And in that moment, his sole purpose became bringing her pleasure. Hearing her voice break on his name. Feeling that flutter of her muscles around the fingers he slid inside her.

Her hands grabbed his head, her hips undulating in a wild rhythm that seemed to demand and beg for the release she hovered on the verge of. With a purse of his lips over the stiff nub of flesh cresting the top of her sex and two hard thrusts into her, she toppled into that release. Trembling thighs squeezed his head. Pleasure-thick cries spilled into the room. Her flavor flowed onto his tongue.

This was heaven, his place of sanctuary.

Nothing could touch him here while he was between her legs.

Hunger surged hotter, fiercer inside him, churning in his gut, pounding in his cock. In lightning-quick movements, he stripped his clothes off, only pausing to grab his wallet and remove a condom from it.

He palmed the protection, and though his body roared for relief, to be buried deep inside the flesh his mouth and fingers had just enjoyed, he didn't rip the foil open. Lifting his gaze to hers, he cupped her cheek and rubbed his thumb over her bottom lip. God, he couldn't get enough of her mouth. To prove it, he leaned forward and, as gently as the lust raging through him would allow, kissed her.

"You can get up and leave if this isn't what you want," he offered, though if she backed out, he might just lose his mind.

"I want this," she whispered, shifting her hand to his dick. Giving him a tight, hard squeeze that propelled the breath from his lungs. He briefly closed his eyes and ground his teeth, giving himself over to the pleasure that careened through him at the long strokes of her hand. "I want you inside me."

He carefully nudged her hand aside and tore open the condom wrapper, swiftly sheathing himself. Weaving their fingers together and nabbing a pillow, he guided her off the couch to the floor. The plush carpet cushioned his knees as he crouched over her. Brown eyes

steadily met his, and he didn't look away as he fisted his
cock and notched himself at her entrance. He watched
her, studying her features for any sign of discomfort, of
pain. But she didn't flinch as he pressed deeper, surging forward. No, it was he who closed his eyes as the
wet, tight heat of her parted for him, embraced him.
Broke him.

He shuddered, fighting not to plunge inside her, to
rut over her like a beast concerned with only his own
gratification. Jesus, he wasn't even all the way inside
her, and he shook with the need to come.

"Ross." Charlotte slid a hand over his tense shoulder,
up the side of his neck and cradled his jaw. "Look at
me." He lifted his lashes, and the sight of her damp lips,
flushed cheeks and glazed eyes worsened the struggle
for control. "I'm not fragile. Take what you need from
me. I can handle it."

He blew out a hard, ragged breath, buried his face in
the crook of her neck—and slammed inside her.

Twin moans filled the room, his dark rumble and her
lighter whimper. Fuck, she... A tremble worked over
him. She was so damn perfect. Strong. Delicate. Wet.
Hot. She was *everything*.

With a growl he couldn't contain, he drew his hips
back and thrust forward, powering into her in a greedy
stroke. She rose to meet him, her legs wrapping around
his hips, and he burrowed impossibly deeper. Palming
her ass, he lifted her into him, riding her, grinding into
her, burying himself over and over because he couldn't
bear not being balls deep inside the heart of her.

She chanted his name, her nails digging into his

back, scratching him. *Marking* him. Yes. God, yes. He wanted that physical claim of ownership—

He shook his head, his mind rebelling at the thought even as he owned her body. Not ownership. Pleasure. He wanted the physical evidence that he could render her mindless with his touch, his cock. Nothing else mattered.

Gritting his teeth, he levered off her, sliding his arms underneath her thighs and hiking them higher, spreading her wider. He pistoned into her, the sound of damp skin slapping together, of his grunts and her moans littering the air. Electric currents sizzled and snapped up and down his spine, even the soles of his feet. But he held on, fought the surge of ecstasy that heralded an orgasm that might take him out of here. Not without her, though.

Reaching between them, he swept his thumb over the top of her sex, circling the little nub of flesh. Circling, then pressing. Hard.

Charlotte stiffened, her back arching hard, her beautiful breasts pointed toward the ceiling. Unable to resist the lure of them, he bowed over her, sucking a nipple deep, thrusting and riding out the orgasm that clutched her in its powerful grasp. A strangled cry escaped her, and she shook, her sex clamping down on him in a bruising grip. Yes, dammit. He wanted to be bruised, to still feel that steel-and-silk clasp tomorrow.

As her tremors started to subside, he gave his own needs free rein. Releasing her breast with a soft pop, he reared back and let go. Each thrust shoved him closer to that crumbling, death-defying edge. Until he just leaped. Bone-cracking pleasure punched into him, and as the orgasm barreled over him, he didn't fight it.

Didn't fight the rapture.

Didn't fight her.

Didn't fight himself.

He surrendered, and for tonight—for this moment—it was all right.

Ten

Ross stood at the window of the Texas Cattleman's Club meeting room, and a sense of déjà vu whispered over him. Hell, had it only been a few weeks since he'd stood here with his father, siblings and Billy, signing the contract for Soiree on the Bay? So much had happened since then. He'd bumped into the woman who'd haunted him for three years, had discovered he was a father and had been disinherited. He shook his head. And to think, when he'd been finalizing those documents, all he'd seen ahead of him was money, success and partying.

Scoffing lightly, he turned and headed to the serving set the club staff had laid out on the small conference table. He poured himself a cup of coffee and sipped, glancing down at his watch. A couple of minutes before one. His stomach twisted, and he clenched his jaw. Another thing that had changed. Never had nerves attacked him at the thought of seeing his sister and brother. They were his best friends—no, more than that. When people survived wars together, that made them closer than blood because their relationship was forged in conflict, battle and grief. Rusty's marriages and divorces had been combat they'd endured, their childhood the battlefield where the three of them had bonded.

But in the week since Rusty had disinherited Ross, he hadn't heard much from his brother and sister. Most of that distance could be placed on his own shoulders. He'd been so busy finding a home for Charlotte, Ben and himself as well as shoring up his own financial resources that he hadn't prioritized sitting down and talking with them. Also, a part of him had subconsciously put off this meeting. Because that part feared where they stood in this face-off between him and Rusty. Gina and Asher had always been his allies, but at the risk of incurring Rusty's wrath?

He didn't know. And he dreaded finding out.

The door to the room opened, and Gina and Asher walked in. Ross stood at the end of the table, tension drawing him tight, unfamiliar indecision humming through him. He studied their faces, searching for… what? Anger? Sadness? Resignation? Did they resent him for making them choose a side…

"Dammit, Ross," Gina snapped, striding forward and not stopping until she threw her arms around him and held on. Relief poured out of him like a geyser, almost sapping his strength. He wrapped his sister in an embrace that was probably too tight, but he couldn't ease up. Not when he'd never been so grateful for a hug. "Where the hell have you been?" A smile curved his mouth at her muffled scolding. "We've been worried sick about how you've been doing, and all we can get out of you is a 'fine' or an 'I'll call you back.' Which you don't do, by the way."

Gina tilted her head back, glaring at him. "Good thing you arranged this meeting because I was ready to storm The Bellamy." She lightly punched him in the arm. "And thank goodness for the Royal gossip hotline or I wouldn't even have known where you were staying."

"She was actually ready to barge in five days ago," Asher added, voice dry but holding an unmistakable affection for their sister. "I convinced her to wait since you had a lot going on—you know, new family and being disinherited—but we didn't intend on waiting too much longer."

Asher clapped Ross on the shoulder, giving it a brief squeeze. His tone might have been amused, but concern darkened his brown eyes. Ross gave him a small nod, which his brother returned before picking up a cup and pouring coffee into it.

"Gina, quit making like a clingy octopus and release Ross. Here." He passed her the cup and fixed another for himself, a brief grin flashing across his face as she switched the glare from Ross to him. "Okay, Ross. Tell us what the hell is going on. We've heard Dad's rant about your ungratefulness, stupidity, disloyalty to family and being led around by your dick." He sipped the fragrant brew. "Now, what's the truth?"

Ross arched an eyebrow, that vise around his chest

loosening at his brother's sardonic words. "How do you know that's not the truth?"

Asher snorted. "When Rusty starts trying to curry favor with me instead of treating me like the unwanted, redheaded stepchild, then I know he's full of shit. And he wants something. That something being getting me on his side to pressure you into caving and falling back into line. Which, even if you weren't my brother, would've put me firmly in your camp."

"Same here. Since you've been banned from the office, he's acting like he actually cares about my input on business decisions. When we both know he doesn't respect my opinions—never has. He's in full-on bribe mode." Gina shook her head, disgust curling her mouth. "As if we're so stupid we can't see right through his manipulations."

Or desperate enough for his attention and his approval that they would turn on him. That was how Rusty Edmond operated in business and with his children.

"So give," Gina prodded. "And start from why we're just finding out we're an aunt and uncle."

Ross did as they requested. And with the two people he trusted most in the world, he confessed everything that had happened since that moment he and Billy had spotted Charlotte in Sheen. By the time he finished with discovering he'd been locked out of the ranch, his credit cancelled and then being swiftly tossed out of the family business, they'd all sunk onto the couch in the meeting room's small sitting area.

"If I doubted Dad's seriousness, the package he had delivered to The Bellamy would've confirmed it. It included a letter stating I was not welcome at Elegance

Ranch and fired from The Edmond Organization, along with the newest copy of his will with me cut out of it. Congratulations, by the way." He shifted his gaze from the empty coffee cup to shoot his sister a wry smile. "You're now the recipient of the majority shares of the company and his estate."

"Awesome," she drawled. But no humor lightened her troubled gaze. "A son, Ross. You have a little boy," she whispered. "How are you handling that?"

He inhaled a breath, then slowly released it, leaning back against the chair. "Gina, Ben is…" He shook his head, his first real smile of the day curving his mouth. "He's beautiful. And amazing. At two, he's so smart and funny. I didn't think I could love someone so quick and so much. But…" He swallowed. "I do. Crazy, I know."

"No, not crazy." Gina covered his hand with hers, eyes gleaming. "You just sound like a father. And I'm so happy for you."

"I am, too," Asher said, leaning forward in his chair and perching his forearms on his thighs. "And what about Charlotte? How do you feel about her?"

Ross didn't reply; instead, he stood and crossed the room back to the table and the serving set. Yes, he freely admitted to stalling a reply to his brother's question. Because while his love for his son was uncomplicated and easy, his feelings toward Charlotte weren't nearly as cut and dried. Did he love her? No, because in order to love someone, to make a commitment to them, you had to trust them. And as much as his dick hardened for her, he didn't trust her.

But the need for her, the lust that hadn't abated just because he'd been inside her again… That muddied what should've been a simple co-parenting arrangement. Instead of satisfying his craving for her, that night at The Bellamy had only intensified it. And though he could list a thousand reasons why he should maintain a platonic relationship with Charlotte, he hadn't heeded them. Neither of them had. They hadn't discussed the ramifications of continuing a co-parenting-with-benefits arrangement, but each night that he stayed at the house with her and Ben or they came to him at the resort, they gave in to the need.

If he was a better man, he wouldn't take advantage. If he was a prouder man, he would demand more of himself. But when it came to Charlotte Jarrett, he was neither.

"She's Ben's mother," he finally said, staring at the dark stream of brew as it flowed into his cup. "We've come to an arrangement that works for both of us. For the next year, we're going to give living together a try. After that, we'll see."

"Now you know that's not what he was asking." Gina snorted. "But that nonanswer was answer enough." Moments later, she appeared at his elbow, cupping it. "What about Dad? Do you plan on trying to approach him again? In case we haven't made it clear, Asher and I are on your side. Just tell us what you need from us."

Ross encircled his sister's shoulder, giving her a small hug of gratitude. "Thank you for that. Both of you," he added, glancing over his shoulder at Asher, who rose from his chair. "But I don't want you to get involved. This is between me and Dad. I don't want you to be casualties in the fallout."

"How are you doing moneywise?" Asher interjected

when Gina frowned and parted her lips, prepared to object to Ross's request. He joined them at the table and shot their sister a look, gently shaking his head. "Can we help you there?"

"No, I'm good," Ross said, grateful for his brother's intervention. He meant it; he didn't want his brother and sister's lives affected by his decisions. Rusty could be vindictive, and though Asher was older than Ross, he had to protect him and Gina from their father's possible retaliation. "I have investments in several companies, stock and connections that aren't tangled up in The Edmond Organization. And I still have Soiree on the Bay. The contracts have been signed. Dad can't kick me out of that like he did from the company."

If anything, being fired had forced Ross to rely only on himself. Thank God, he'd diversified his own funds years ago, not living completely off the family business. He wasn't a pauper by any stretch of the imagination. Hell, according to his financial portfolio, he was still a millionaire in his own right. But… Unease coiled inside his chest. But he might not have enough on-hand cash to pay Charlotte the five hundred thousand he'd promised her.

"I hate that you're going through this," Gina hissed, crossing her arms over her chest. "While I'm pissed at Dad, I can't say I'm surprised. Just look how he treated Mom when she dared to defy him."

Ross stiffened, an old but very familiar anger kindling in his veins. "This situation is completely different from that."

"Not by much," his sister argued. "She asked Dad for a divorce, and he went after her with everything he had. Forget that she was the mother of his children. He kicked her out of her house, changed the locks, made it difficult for her to see her children. He took everything that was important from her."

"She chose a big settlement over her children," he snapped. "No one forced her to leave Royal, to leave us. She divorced Dad, not us. I've only had Ben in my life for a matter of weeks, but I would do anything for that little boy. Destroy anyone who tried to hurt him. You fight for those you love. *Sarabeth*," he uttered her name on a mocking sneer, because she hadn't been Mom to him a long time, "chose to walk away. To not be in our lives except for the occasional visit or phone call. If she truly wanted to be there for us, no power in this world, including the long arm of Rusty Edmond, could've kept her away. So no, it's not similar at all."

Asher edged closer to their sister, clasping her hand in his, and Ross pivoted away, suddenly feeling like an ogre. His issues with his mother were just that— his issues. He had no right to jump down Gina's throat because she chose to see the woman who'd essentially abandoned them in a kinder light.

"When was the last time you saw her, Ross? Spoke to her?" Gina asked softly.

"Years. And I'm fine with maintaining the status quo."

"You should call her. Talk to her. I think you would be surprised with the answers she could give you."

Answers? Could her *answers* turn back time and give him her much-needed presence in his life? Could they make up for her absence? For her rejection of him? For making him question his own self-worth? How could he be worthy of anything when the two people who were supposed to love him unconditionally had rejected him at every turn? His mother had chosen freedom over him, and his father—fuck, Rusty was Rusty. Everything had come before Ross, Gina and Asher. Business, women, a goddamn prize bull. The man had missed Ross's college graduation because of a cattle sale. And now, he put his pride before his son.

No. He didn't need to ask Sarabeth anything. Her absence and Rusty's emotional deprivation had been enough of a very thorough explanation.

"I'm through talking about her," Ross said, a sudden bone-deep weariness creeping into his voice. "Do you two want to meet your nephew?"

He'd brought Ben with him to the clubhouse and left him in the day care while he met with Gina and Asher.

"Of course." Gina crossed over to him and wrapped him in a hug. "I'm sorry for bringing up Mom and pressuring you," she murmured.

"No worries." He pressed a kiss to the top of her head.

"Let's go," Asher said. "I want to officially meet my nephew. You said he's beautiful. So that means he must take after his mother."

Ross met his brother's smirk and grinned. "Asshole."

Asher laughed, pulling the meeting room door open. "Well, that's a family trait, so let's *really* hope he takes after his mother."

Gina gasped in mock outrage. "I beg your pardon," she objected as she swept past Asher into the hallway. "Speak for yourself. I merely know my own mind and am not afraid to let others know it, as well."

Asher tilted his head. "Huh. When I do that, I'm always called an asshole."

Ross chuckled, following his brother and sister—his family—toward the front of the building.

God, he loved them.

Eleven

"This is ridiculous," Charlotte grumbled, staring at herself in the closet mirror.

Hah. As if the space that was bigger than her bedroom in her former home could be called something as simple as a *closet*. She didn't even have enough clothes to fill all the drawers, racks and hangers. Not to mention the stacks of mini cases meant to store jewelry. Besides the pair of diamond studs that was a graduation gift from her parents and the necklace Ross had given her, she only owned costume jewelry that would look laughable in those boxes.

Speaking of the necklace... She grazed fingertips over the heart-shaped pendant, then removed it, laying it on the island behind her. So far, she'd done a good job of keeping it hidden from Ross even though they now lived together.

And slept together.

No, that wasn't exactly correct.

They had sex and then went their separate ways to their separate bedrooms.

Then, in the morning, they pretended they were nothing more than Ben's parents. Cordial strangers who happened to share the same space. Sometime between his meeting with his brother and sister at the TCC clubhouse and that evening when she'd returned home from work, he'd grown distant, unfailingly polite—colder. But just with her.

With Ben, he was simply wonderful. After Ben was born, and Charlotte had faced those nights of midnight feedings, crying, explosive diapers and runny noses alone, she'd wondered how different things could've been if Ross were there. If she'd had someone to share the load. And now she didn't have to imagine. As aloof as he was with her, Ross poured all of his affection into their son. Even her parents, who'd been understandably shocked and confused when she'd confessed about Ross being Ben's father, respected Ross for how he'd stepped up and taken to parenthood with an obvious enthusiasm. Though Charlotte's unease about forever being connected in some way to Rusty and her fear of his retaliation hadn't faded, she couldn't deny Ben adored his father.

She also couldn't deny her growing feelings for Ross.

Stupid. Stupid. Stupid.

She mentally slapped her palm to her forehead over and over. As if that could shake some latent sense of self-preservation loose.

What was it with her continually falling for the same unavailable and totally inappropriate man? What did that say about her? What was it about herself that made her believe she wasn't worthy of a man who would put her first, be proud to claim her as his own, be fully committed to her?

For most of her life, she'd longed for a relationship like her parents. Total devotion. Yet, the first time she'd fallen in love, it was with a man who'd been okay with keeping her a secret from his family, his friends, the world. Yes, she'd had her reasons for agreeing to the clandestine affair, too. But deep inside, where the most vulnerable desires of her heart hid, she'd longed for him to say, "fuck that," and shout his delight in being with her to anyone who would listen. Just as she'd longed for him to stop her from going to California, to ask her to stay for him. For *them*.

She'd promised herself she'd never place herself in that predicament again. But now, here she stood. In a gorgeous home she could never afford on her own, in the exclusive, gated community of Pine Valley, living with Ross Edmond as his baby's mother. Falling for the same man again.

And her love for him was still a secret.

"You look beautiful."

Her head jerked up, heart pounding a double-time cadence. Ross leaned against the doorway, a shoulder propped against the jamb, hands in the pockets of his black tuxedo pants. As if her body had a "clap on" switch, just the sight of him had her belly clenching, lust lighting up her veins like the Vegas strip, and her sex pulsing.

Dammit. She returned her gaze to her reflection in the mirror, but that didn't eradicate the image of him from her brain. Dirty blond hair tamed and waving away from his stunning face erected of strong, arrogant angles and carnal curves. Tall, big body clothed in a white shirt, bow tie and pants that showcased the lean, muscular perfection of his frame. She intimately knew the strength of that body. Knew how he could restrain and unleash its power.

A curl of heat spiraled through her, whispering over her nipples and winding down to the empty, aching flesh between her thighs. Deliberately, she reminded herself that he'd probably uttered those same words to hundreds of women.

The compliment wasn't anything special to him— and neither was she.

"Thank you," she said, giving herself a mental fist pump when her voice emerged even, unaffected. "Although that has more to do with the dress—which you would know since you had it sent over," she added dryly.

The deep purple, sequin-embellished, floor-length gown skimmed over her curves like a lover's caress. The wide dolman-style sleeves cuffed at her wrists, and the neckline plunged to a point beneath her breasts. A skinny belt of the same material cinched her middle, emphasizing the indent of her waist.

It was the most beautiful, expensive thing she'd ever owned besides the necklace he'd given her.

He moved fully into the closet and appeared behind her in the mirror. At five foot eight, she wasn't a short woman, but he dwarfed her. And then quickly, a visual of them from the night before flashed in her head. Her, on her hands and knees. Him, behind her, covering her...

She briefly closed her eyes, but the image burned brighter, hotter. When she opened her eyes, they clashed with Ross's hooded, ice-blue gaze. No, not ice. Heat and smoke.

Tension filled the closet, winding around them, and she could feel the stroke of his perusal over the skin bared by the daring neckline. She tried to smother the shiver working its way through her body. Tried and failed.

Apprehension that was purely feminine flared inside her, and she could do nothing but watch him. Wait for his next move. Half hope, half dread he would strip her of the dress and take her down to the closet floor and ease the sensual pain spasming in her sex.

Strip her of her dignity while he was at it.

"What's ridiculous?" he asked.

She blinked. Relief and disappointment cascaded through her, and she quickly recovered, running their conversation back in her head and realizing he must've been standing in the closet doorway longer than she'd noticed.

"All of this." She waved a hand from the top of her hair, which the stylist had fashioned into an elegant yet edgy Mohawk, and down her body, encompassing the gown. "I'm a chef. Not a socialite. I should be at my restaurant, cooking on a Saturday night, not attending some party. The most talking I do is giving orders in the kitchen and meeting customers tableside. And even then, I try to keep it as short as possible. This—" she once more flicked a hand up and down her frame "—isn't me."

"How do you know?" he countered, shifting closer

so his chest brushed her spine. "Maybe this is just an aspect of who you are. Your dream is to become a master chef. That could take you around the world, to television, to endorsements. And all of that requires socializing with people, selling yourself. Consider this a training ground for the future." His words painted a picture she'd dreamed of, craved. She lifted her gaze from her neckline to meet his eyes. Did he believe she could obtain that future? Did he believe in...her? A merciless hand squeezed her heart, and she silently cursed herself for even caring about his opinion—caring about his esteem. She *was* enough, dammit!

"And Jeremy obviously thinks the same, since he approved and fully supported you attending this *party*." His lips twisted into a sardonic smile around her terminology for the swank event scheduled for this evening. "He understands you are the face of Sheen and the connection with Soiree on the Bay will only increase his profile in Royal as well as nationally, perhaps internationally."

He skimmed the backs of his fingers down her cheek, dropping to caress her throat before lowering his arm back to his side. Her skin pulsed and tingled from the contact as if it'd been sunburned.

"Besides, Brett Harston, Lila Jones and Valencia Donovan will be there," he added, referring to the other members of the advisory board.

Since joining the board, Charlotte had become friends with the other members. She snorted. If anyone had told her just a month ago that she could claim a self-made millionaire, a Chamber of Commerce employee and the founder of a charity as friends, she would've escorted them to a waiting Uber with an admonition about drinking too much.

But here she was, chummy with members of Royal high society, wearing a gown that probably cost more than her car down payment, and getting ready to attend an event at the famed Texas Cattleman's Club.

She sighed, about to rub her damp palms down her thighs, but catching herself at the last minute. *This dress isn't your food-splattered chef jacket*, she silently scolded.

"Well, I'm as ready as I'll ev—"

"What's this?"

She turned at Ross's harsh bark, and her throat spasmed, trapping her breath. Seemingly of their own accord, her fingers drifted to her bare neck, where the necklace currently clenched in his fist had rested minutes earlier.

"I—" She couldn't squeeze anything else past her constricted throat.

God, she'd been so careful. Hadn't expected him to show up in her room or her closet. But none of her intentions mattered now. Not with that arctic glare pinning her to the spot and his body so taut he practically vibrated with the blast of frigid rage rolling off him.

"Why do you still have this?" he demanded in a low, dark tone that rumbled with…emotion. Not just anger. Something else—something almost raw—threaded through it. And though she couldn't identify it, she trembled underneath it. "Charlotte," Ross growled.

She jerked at the sound of her name, dragging her gaze from the dangling pendant and chain to once more meet his stare. And try not to flinch from it.

"It's mine," she said. "You gave it to me."

"I know that, dammit," he snapped. "I remember everything I ever gave you. *Everything*. And when you ran away to California, you left it all. I went into the guesthouse afterward. It was empty except for all of the earrings, bracelets, clothes I'd given you. Like they were a message you wanted to make sure I received. That they—like me—meant nothing. Just trash to throw away once you were done with them."

With me.

He didn't utter those two words, but they echoed between them as if they'd been shouted at the top of his lungs.

"That's not true," she whispered. Leaving those things behind had been a desperate act of self-protection. It had been her survival instinct kicking in. She couldn't take any reminder of him with her to California. Because they would've been torture, constant souvenirs from a time when she'd been at her happiest—when she'd been fatalistically and foolishly in love. She couldn't keep those pieces of him and make a new life for herself absent of him.

Little had she known that she'd left with the most permanent of reminders inside her.

"Then what is the truth? Did this accidentally make the journey to California?" He chuckled, the serrated edge of it pricking her skin, her heart.

"Actually, yes," she admitted. "I didn't know it was in my suitcase until I arrived there." She clearly remembered that moment when she'd found the jewelry in her carry-on. Remembered how she'd broken down, curled on the bed, clutching it to her chest. How ironic that the pendant was heart-shaped, when hers had been shattered so completely.

"And yet you kept it? Why not pawn it? Believe me, it would've brought you a pretty penny. Several hundred thousand of them," he scoffed, the corner of his mouth pulling into a cruel smile. "Why, Charlotte? For once, give me a straight answer."

"What are you angry at, Ross?" she asked, forcing herself to face that stare that both froze her blood and heated it. "Why do you care?"

"You left," he accused in a low roar.

And there it was. The crux of why he would never forgive her. Not for having a baby he'd known nothing about. Not for missing out on two years of his son's life. No, she'd had the audacity to walk away from him before he could do the honors. To take his favorite toy of the moment away from him when he hadn't been finished playing.

If her heart hadn't already been battered, scarred and calcified, it might've broken all over again.

"I'm sorry," she replied, and surprise flickered in his narrowed stare. "I apologize for not remaining in Royal as your dirty secret. Please forgive me for being exhausted with remaining here as someone you hid out of shame."

She drew her shoulders back and tilted her chin higher, desperately grasping for an aloof mask that concealed the pain throbbing inside her like an open wound.

"You want a straight answer? Okay. You're right. I could've thrown the necklace away or pawned it. God knows the money I could've gotten for it would've helped. But I didn't. I kept it because every time I saw it, touched it, I remembered that for almost a year I allowed myself to be involved in an affair that demeaned me. That I lowered my personal standards to become the plaything of a man who deemed me good enough for a fuck but not to escort past the kitchen. Every time I wear that necklace it's a reminder to myself to never repeat that mistake. A reminder that I'm worth more than being a receptacle for a rich man's lust."

The air crackled with their fury, her hurt, her pain. The bitterness of her words lay acrid on her tongue, leaving a grimy residue that no amount of mouthwash—or apologies—could rinse clean.

I didn't mean it.

The cry screamed inside her like a banshee. It wailed in her head, begging her to say it. But she couldn't. Because part of her—that lonely, pregnant woman who'd felt betrayed by the man she'd loved—had meant every festering word.

"At least we know where we stand with each other," Ross finally said into the thick, deafening silence. "Here." He dropped the necklace on the island, the pendant clacking against the marble top. "I wouldn't want you to lose it." Turning on his heel, he strode toward the closet door. And she curled her fingers into her palms, convincing herself she didn't want to stroke the rigid line of his spine. Or brush a caress over the perfectly cut hair above the collar of his shirt. "Let me know when you're ready. We can't be late," he instructed without glancing back at her.

Then he disappeared through the door, leaving her alone.

Except for the echo of her cruel words.

Twelve

"How're you enjoying yourself, Charlotte?" Billy Holmes appeared at her elbow, holding two glasses of wine.

Giving Ross's friend and business partner a smile, she accepted one of the flutes and immediately sipped. Alcoholic fortification was an absolute must to get through this night.

"What's not to enjoy?" she replied, glancing around the crowded, cavernous great room.

Whoever Ross and Billy hired to decorate needed a fat tip. The designer had turned what could've been an austere room with its cross-beamed cathedral ceiling and dark wood floors into a winter wonderland. White lights and flowers with boughs of greenery wound around tall pillars and along the massive fireplace.

Crystal centerpieces adorned the round tables and mini trees painted white, and entwined with more lights, added an almost fairy-tale air. And strategically placed in all that ethereal beauty were brochures, pamphlets and even samples from Soiree on the Bay's attending vendors, sponsors and the charities benefiting from the donations. Before she'd left work earlier, she'd overseen the samples from Sheen—an Alaskan king crab cake with a sweet and spicy roulade sauce and squares of ham, feta and sweet potato quiche. Last time she'd checked, there'd only been a few dishes left of each.

As if reading her mind, Billy murmured, "Great wine. Great food." He cocked his head. "Your samples have disappeared, and dinner hasn't even been served yet. I'd claim that as a ringing endorsement of Sheen and its chef. Congratulations." He toasted her with his glass and grinned, his blue eyes gleaming. "Far be it from me to brag, but I unashamedly accept full credit for bringing you into the fold."

Charlotte chuckled. "Well, I'm so glad you're above an 'I told you so,'" she drawled. "I admit, I had my reservations about joining the festival, but they've mostly been laid to rest. This is a great move for Sheen."

"And for you, Charlotte," Billy added, briefly cupping her elbow before dropping his arm back to his side. "A restaurant is only as strong as its chef, and your reputation as an extraordinary culinary artist precedes you. So thank you for taking a leap with us."

She nodded, unsure how to respond to the outpouring of praise. Ross's words from earlier floated through her head. *Consider this a training ground for the fu-*

ture. According to him, she belonged here, receiving compliments as her due.

Of course, that had been before the blowup that had decimated all the ground they'd recovered.

Billy cleared his throat, and stared down into his glass, lightly swirling the wine. "Charlotte," he murmured, lifting his head to meet her gaze. "I don't mean to pry, but Ross is my best friend. And I can't help but notice there seems to be some—" he hesitated "—*distance* between you two tonight. Is everything okay?"

The "We're fine" danced on her tongue, but it lodged in her throat, the lie refusing to be uttered. Instead, she avoided that concerned scrutiny under the pretense of surveying the room. And inevitably, her perusal landed on Ross. Surrounded by his brother, sister and a small crowd, he appeared to be the charming, charismatic playboy she'd always known. Not a care in the world. As she watched, a beautiful brunette in a slinky gold dress inched up to his side and laid a hand on his arm. He bowed his head over her, and—

Nope. She turned away, raising her glass for a healthy gulp of wine. Not even going to do it to herself.

"That's the daughter of one of our largest investors besides The Edmond Organization. Believe me, there's nothing inappropriate going on between them," Billy said, his gentle tone almost painful.

Was she that obvious?

How could Ross's friend see what she tried so hard to hide?

"Doesn't matter," she replied, and the smile she forced felt brittle to her own self. "Ross and I are just co-parents. He's free to do whatever—or whomever—he wants."

"As long as I've known Ross, things have seemed to come easy to him. Most definitely because of his last name and family. Then add in his looks, which would make a lesser man completely insecure," he said, flashing her a smile, "and a magnetism that just seems to draw people to him, and he hasn't had to struggle. Not that I'm implying he isn't a hard worker, because he is. But it hasn't been until you came back to Royal and he learned about Ben that he's been truly challenged for the first time in his life. And he's risen to it. Being a father has given him new purpose, and yet, I can't imagine how scary all of this must be for him. So please, as his friend, I'm asking you not to give up on him. You and Ben, you're good for him."

"Yes, we're so good for Ross that his father disinherited him because of us," she said, battling back the warmth that skated too close to hope. "Did you see the two of them tonight? Rusty barely spared Ross a glance."

Billy sighed, slipping a hand in his front pocket. "I admire Rusty. He's a brilliant businessman, and no one can deny that. But the personality that makes him a force to be reckoned with in the industry is also the same personality that he brings to his family. C'mon, Charlotte, you worked in that house, you've been around the family enough to know there were issues way before now. They'll get through this—they're strong, and underneath the stubbornness is an abundance of love. But I don't know if Ross will make it without you and

Ben. You two were the catalyst for this change, and he needs you."

He shrugged a shoulder. "Like I said, I don't know what happened between you two before tonight, but my friend is more focused and happier than he's been in a long time. So again, please hang in there with him. Don't give up."

Billy squeezed her hand, then walked away, his plea echoing in her head.

My friend is more focused and happier than he's been in a long time... Don't give up.

There was so much between her and Ross—too much. Mistrust. Hurt. Resentment. Insecurity. As their argument earlier in the closet proved.

And yet... She glanced across the room and unerringly sought him out. Though still surrounded by people, for once, a smile didn't curve his mouth. Someone wasn't commanding his attention. He stood there, an island in a sea of admirers, hangers-on and wannabe lovers. Alone. Untouchable. Lonely. Did any of them truly see the real man behind the tuxedo, the magnetism, the playboy exterior? The man who longed for a domineering father's approval and concealed a wounded heart behind an indifferent demeanor? The man who'd unconditionally accepted a son he hadn't known about and loved him without reserve.

No, none of them saw *that* man. But she'd been gifted with glimpses of him. And those glimpses only made her crave more of him. Made her yearn for the impossible.

That he would someday give her the same uninhibited love he so freely offered Ben.

What would it be like to love him without fear of rejection, without baggage from the past, without dread that outside forces would come between them? With the security that she was enough?

It would be the kind of dream that slowly faded when morning arrived, but which she desperately tried to cling to even if only for a few sacred moments.

As if he felt her gaze on him, Ross glanced up, and their eyes met. And even though a room separated them, she reeled from the intensity of that stare. In spite of the harmful words she'd hurled at him earlier, she needed to feel connected to him. Needed to somehow work toward erasing the distance that she'd placed between them.

God, she just needed him.

Heart thumping against her sternum, she tipped her head to the side, hoping he understood her message to follow her. Not waiting lest she lose her nerve to go through with this, she turned and slipped out one of the side doors. She walked past several closed doors, and randomly choosing one that was far enough away from the great room, she twisted the knob and entered. A large and curtainless picture window dominated one wall, allowing moonlight to stream through and illuminate what appeared to be a private and informal meeting room. A stone fireplace, several big armchairs, a small couch and a couple of coffee tables filled the space.

She didn't make it past the first chair when the door opened behind her and clicked shut. Inhaling a breath, she held it for several seconds, and then slowly released it, pivoting to face Ross. In the semidark, his large frame loomed larger, and her belly fluttered. With his impassive expression, he betrayed nothing of his thoughts or emotions. But he was here. And she'd take that as a positive sign.

"Ross," she began, then stopped. Because she had no idea what to say. *I just needed you to look* at *me and not* through *me* didn't seem like a good opener. She shook her head, tried again. "Ross, I wanted to apologize. About earlier. This night is important to you, and what happened between us threw a pall over it that doesn't belong. I'm sorry for that."

"Is that what you and Billy were talking about?"

She blinked, taken aback by the abrupt question. "No," she said. "Well, not really…"

"Which is it?" he pressed in the low, quiet tone that still set her instinctive alarm system clanging. "Because it looked like a serious conversation, given the way you two were cozied up together."

She frowned, lifting her hands. "Wait. What the hell is going on here?"

"He asked would I mind if he asked you out. Did I ever tell you that?" He stepped away from the door, stalking closer to her. "After he first met you at Sheen," he continued, not granting her the chance to reply. "He called you beautiful and wanted you."

"What did you tell him?" she breathed, still unsure of what was happening but rapidly getting tugged down by the undertow of desire swirling around them.

Ross might appear the epitome of cool composure, but his eyes… They burned bright. Anger? Lust? Didn't matter, because both caused the air to snag in her lungs, dampened her palms and beaded her nipples into tight points, setting off a pulsing throb in her sex.

Jesus, what did that say about her?

Nothing flattering.

"I told him to go for it." He moved even closer. And closer still, until the lapels of his tuxedo jacket grazed the tips of her breasts. She just managed to swallow a gasp. "I didn't know you were the mother of my son then, but the reason still stands. We're sometimes acquaintances, sometimes enemies. Co-parents who want nothing from each other but the best for our son. We're a mistake that are now connected for the next sixteen years, right?"

"Ross," she whispered, voice breaking. "I'm—"

"Sorry," he finished, flicking a hand, the gold of his watch glinting in the shadowed room. "You said that. Did Billy flirt with you? Ask you how we were doing?"

"Yes, but not how you're insinuating," she objected, frowning.

He arched an eyebrow, and the mocking gesture sparked a flame of irritation. "Really? And what am I insinuating?" he drawled.

"If I didn't know better—and believe me, I do—I'd swear you were jealous. Which is ridiculous considering you were just out there with women not just hanging from your every word, but from *you*," she snapped.

Shit.

She didn't lose her temper often, but dammit, when she did, her mouth ran like a swollen spring river—fast, babbling and all over the place.

"And if I didn't know better, I'd think that was jealousy," he taunted, cocking his head and peering down at her through a thick fringe of lashes. "Fortunately, I know better, too. But just in case you need clarification, other than how they can benefit the festival, I don't give a damn about those women. And I definitely don't want to fuck them. You're the only one I need to be inside of. The only one who can get me hard just by breathing." He tunneled his fingers through the fall of her hair and tugged, yanking her head back so his mouth hovered over hers. "And you're wrong, Charlotte." He pulled harder, and she sank her teeth into her bottom lip, trapping the groan that almost slipped free at the corresponding tingle across her scalp. "I am jealous. Two times Billy touched you. And both times I battled back the urge to rush across the room and shove him against the wall and away from you."

Shock crackled through her, the static of it convincing her she'd misheard. She slowly shook her head. "You don't—"

"Mean it?" he interrupted her once more, completing her sentence. "Yes, I do. To you, I might be a mistake," he repeated what she'd called him again for the second time in as many minutes, and it shredded her. "But to all of them out there, including my friend, you're mine. At night, when you're under me, moaning my name, coming around my dick, you're mine. Aren't you?" He rolled his hips, his erection, thick and hard, grinding against her belly. "Aren't you, baby?"

She squeezed her eyes closed. Trembled. And rasped, "Yes."

His mouth crushed down on hers, consuming the echo of the word and robbing her breath. Hard, rough, hot. Nothing gentle about this kiss. It was pure lust and aggression. Pure need. She shoved her fingers through his hair, fisting the cool strands, her ravenous desire rising to match his.

She didn't give a damn that just down the hallway, hundreds of people congregated. Didn't care that anyone could easily open that door—just as easily as she'd done. No, she didn't spare one more thought on any of that. Everything in her focused on this man devouring her mouth like he'd been on a hunger strike, and she was his first meal.

His arm wrapped around her waist, hauling her tighter to him, and his big frame surrounded her. Protecting her. Even as she tumbled headlong into the wild sexual chaos he never failed to stir within her, she didn't fight or fear it. Not when she had utter confidence that he would be her anchor.

"Put your legs around me," he ordered seconds before hiking her into the air.

She obeyed, wrapping herself around him, trusting his strength, his power. In several long strides, he had her back pressed to the wall. One glance over his shoulder assured her they were steeped in shadow, the pale moonbeams not reaching them in their corner. Of course, Ross would've considered their privacy and her modesty. Even if by chance someone passed by the window that looked out over the lawn and stable, they wouldn't glimpse her and Ross. The knowledge allowed her to sink further into him, under his spell.

With the wall behind her and his body aligned against her front, she was trapped. And didn't want to escape. Cupping his jaw, she settled her thumbs on his chin and tugged. Demanding he open wider for her. Triumph and satisfaction sang through her when he complied, cocking his head so she could thrust deeper, help herself to more of him.

God help her, but she would never get enough of this man. She acknowledged that fact with a fatalistic certainty. She could no more change it than she could who fathered her baby. Ross had imprinted himself on her so long ago, branding her with his special mark of passion, of possession. Maybe it hadn't been time, work and motherhood that had prevented her from becoming romantically involved again in these past three years. Maybe it had been the knowledge that no one else could make her fly and die at the same time.

"Touch me," she pleaded, unashamed in her need. Peppering fevered kisses across his cheek and jaw, she whispered, "Please, touch me."

The night at The Bellamy, it'd been she who'd sought to help him forget with passion. Now she needed him to do the same for her. Help her forget she'd hurt him with her angry words. Help her forget she'd hurt herself.

"Where?" He cupped her breast in his big hand, his thumb rubbing her nipple over her dress. She whimpered, arching into the caress. "Here?"

"No." She wrapped her fingers around his, and with the other hand, tugged the neckline to the side, exposing her bra and flesh. Still not satisfied, she yanked down the cup, freeing herself. "Here."

He bent his head over her, his growl of approval humming against her skin as he sucked her deep. Pulling on her. Licking her. Tormenting her. She rasped nonsensical words as he worked her over. They could've been praise or pleas, she didn't know. Didn't care. Just as long as he kept hauling her to the brink. Here they let down their guards, their swords, and loved.

Or at least she did.

Biting her lip, she clutched his head, lifted it and brought it to the neglected breast. Together, they bared her, and together they offered her up to his voracious mouth. She shook in his arms, undulating wildly, rubbing her sex against his dick. Yes, layers of clothing separated them, but it didn't prevent each stroke and glide from sending more and more pleasure streaking through her. She could come from just this. From just his mouth and fingers and riding his cock.

"Back pocket," he snapped, abandoning her breasts to capture her mouth again. "Get my wallet and take the condom out." Impatient fingers dropped to her thighs, gathering her dress around her hips. "Now, Charlotte."

"No," she breathed, flattening her palms against his chest and pushing. He jerked his head up, his eyes blazing down into hers. She shoved again, and he stepped back, and in spite of the disbelief flaring in his gaze, gently lowered her to the floor. "Not yet."

And she dropped to her knees.

"Fuck." His groan reverberated in the room, and he didn't stop her as she loosened the tab on his pants. Instead he slapped his hands to the wall, looming over her. She tipped her head back, meeting his narrowed stare as she lowered the zipper, dipped her hand inside his black boxer briefs and pulled him free. "Baby, you don't have to do this."

"Yes, I do," she murmured, rubbing a thumb over the swollen and already slick head. "I need this. And so do you."

Without hesitation, she took him inside her. Their twin moans filtered through the air, followed by his sharp bark of pleasure. Or was it pain?

Closing her eyes, she lost herself in the earthy taste, the soft and steely texture, the heavy density of him. How he filled her mouth to overflowing. She fisted the bottom half of his cock, pumping it in a steady rhythm, her lips bumping her fingers on the tail end of each stroke.

"So good," she whispered, dragging her tongue up his length. "I'd forgotten how good you taste."

"Are you trying to make me come right here in this pretty mouth, baby?" He cupped her cheek, the tender gesture belying the roughness of his voice. "Keep talking like that, and I will."

"I want all of you," she confessed on a low rasp before sucking him back in. He probably assumed she meant his sex, his body, the rapture they gave each other. But she didn't. She yearned for *everything*. His body. His touch. His time. His laughter.

His heart.

Even as she pleasured him, tears glinted her eyes. Because part of her knew this would probably be all they could have. Too many words, bruises and wounds stood between them. Too many secrets.

Desperation plowed into her, and to battle it, she swallowed him deeper, his tip hitting the back of her throat.

"Enough," he snarled, jerking free, and cuffing her upper arms he hauled her to her feet. "I want inside you," he muttered, hurriedly removing his wallet and a condom. In moments, he sheathed himself and lifted her back in his arms, his hands cupping her ass. "Take me inside, baby."

Breath blasting in and out of her swollen lips, she

reached between them, encircled his erect flesh, pulled the wet panel of her panties aside and guided it to her entrance. Wrapping her arms around his neck, she lifted herself and sank down. Until all of him was firmly surrounded by her.

Oh, God. She buried her face against his throat. As often as they'd had sex since that first time at The Bellamy, she'd become used to him. But she'd never become used to how completely he filled her. Branded her. *Completed* her.

"Move," she ordered. Begged. "Please, move."

Pressing her harder against the wall, Ross grabbed her hair and tugged her head up. "I want to watch it," he said, his gaze roaming over her face.

She didn't need to ask the definition of "it." Because when his hips drew back, then thrust into her, and she cried out, lips parting, eyes closing, he murmured, "That's it."

He didn't grant her any mercy. Using the leverage of the wall, he slammed into her over and over again, alternating between slow, dirty grinds and hard, abrupt strokes. Each time he buried himself in the core of her, the base of his cock massaged the top of her sex, agitating the bundle of nerves there. The slap of skin punctuated the air along with his grunts and her hoarse cries. He dragged her to the edge of the abyss, and she fought it, then willingly went.

She couldn't breathe. Couldn't think. Couldn't do anything but break.

And God, did she.

She erupted, shaking and seizing in his arms, flinging herself into ecstasy with no care of how she landed.

If she landed. Her sex clamped down on his cock, and his growl echoed in her ear as he drove past her quivering flesh, pursuing his own end. She held on, and though exhaustion pulled at her, she bucked her hips, giving him the same measure he'd gifted her.

Her name, shouted in his raw voice, rebounded off the walls of the room, and she finally wilted against him, confident he wouldn't let her fall.

At least not physically.

Because for her heart, it was too little, too late.

Thirteen

Ross sat in his car in the same parking space that had been his since he'd officially started working for The Edmond Organization six years ago. He snorted. He might've been disinherited and fired, but at least his father hadn't gotten around to reassigning his spot.

Drumming his fingers against the steering wheel, he stared at the building that had been his home away from home. And now he had neither. He sighed, scrubbing a hand down his face.

What the hell was he doing here?

What did he hope to accomplish with this visit?

Immediately, Ben's face drifted across his mind's eye. Before he'd dropped his son off at his grandparents' house for an afternoon visit, Ben had wrapped his arms around his legs, beaming up at him. No hesitation.

No uncertainty. His son was so secure and confident in his father's love that he'd demanded, "Daddy, kiss bye!" without any fear of rejection. Certain he'd receive the affection that was his due.

Ross huffed out a soft chuckle, the sound somehow foreign to him in the silence of the car. As was the prickle of heat behind his rib cage. That free display of love had triggered a yearning in him—a yearning that had driven him here instead of his meeting with Billy. Ben deserved to know all of his family. Especially his grandfather. Maybe he and Rusty hadn't enjoyed a loving relationship, but that didn't mean Ross's son couldn't have that with Rusty.

Though it meant swallowing his pride, he had to try. Not just for his son. But for himself, too.

Resolute, he climbed out the car and headed into the Edmond building. Security had every right to stop him and force him to sign in as a visitor. But the guard on duty only greeted him as Ross walked toward the elevators. Even the pass that only certain personnel possessed to access the executive floor worked. It hadn't been deactivated, as he'd expected.

Frowning, but not questioning his luck—accepting it as fate—he emerged from the elevator onto the hushed floor housing his family's offices. More than a few people did a double take as he strode toward his father's assistant's desk. But he ignored them, focusing instead on the task at hand. Because getting in to see his father without an appointment would be the hugest hurdle.

"Good afternoon, Lisa," he said, smiling at the pretty blonde. "Does Dad have a few minutes available in his schedule for me?"

"Hi, Ross." She offered him a smile in return, though curiosity gleamed in her brown eyes. No doubt wondering what business the disinherited heir could possibly have with his father. She tapped on her keyboard and glanced at her monitor. "He doesn't have a meeting until two, so there's about a half hour free, but—"

"Thanks." He strode past the desk toward the closed double doors. "I'll just go in. No need to announce me."

"But—"

Inside he cringed as he gripped the knob and pushed the door open. That had been an asshole move worthy of a spoiled child, but if he'd allowed her to give Rusty a heads-up that his son wanted to see him, Ross would've spent the rest of the afternoon sitting on one of the couches in the waiting area.

Rusty could carry petty to a whole new level.

His father glanced up at the opening of the door, then scowled. "Ross, what are you doing here?"

Shutting the door behind him, he crossed the huge office, coming to a halt in front of Rusty's desk. He didn't bother taking a seat in one of the visitors' chairs since he most likely wouldn't be here long enough to become comfortable.

"I'm here to see you, Dad. We didn't have a chance to talk Saturday night."

Rusty snorted, tossing down his pen onto his desk. "Is that right? Could be because the rest of us were working while you were up that woman's skirts." His mouth curled into a hard, mocking smile. "Think no one noticed you two disappear? Or that before then, something was off between you? Christ, son, you looked like someone had shot your goddamn dog. Whether you're fucking them or arguing with them, you shouldn't let a woman interfere with business. And you failed on both accounts Saturday."

Heat bloomed beneath his collar, and he slowly dragged in a breath. *You're here to heal the rift, not widen it. You can't tell the old bastard to go to hell.*

The reminder drifted through his head, and after several seconds he could inhale air that wasn't singed by his anger.

"I'm not here to discuss Charlotte," he said.

"What else is there to discuss?" Rusty snapped, slapping his palms to the desk and surging to his feet. "She's at the root of all of this. First, she disrespected my employment and my home by sleeping with my son. Then, she gets pregnant, no doubt on purpose, and when I tell her to get rid of it, she lied about doing that. And then, she has the gall to show up here in Royal again, looking to hook you, an Edmond, with a kid that's her responsibility, not yours, since she made the decision to keep it."

"What kind of man would it make me if I denied my child, abandoned him? That wouldn't make me any better than Sarabeth," he countered.

"Don't bring up that woman's name to me. Your mother was another one who used her children for a big payday and then disappeared. And you can damn well bet that's going to happen with Charlotte," he fumed, jabbing a finger at Ross. "You think you have this happy little family? What happens when she realizes I'm serious about not giving you one red cent, Ross? Do you really believe she's going to stick around? You're being led around by your dick, and I'm not going to stand by and watch it happen. And when she leaves with that boy, I'll be damned if you come crawling back to me."

Each insult barreled into him, delivering strikes to every insecurity and doubt that hid in his subconscious. He was far from penniless, but even with the home he provided for her and Ben, Ross worried it wouldn't be enough. Especially since last week, he'd gone over his finances with his accountant, and as he'd suspected and feared, though he possessed stocks, investments and property, he wouldn't have enough liquid wealth to give her the five-hundred-thousand-dollar payment at the end of their year together. Once he told her the truth, would she pack up Ben and leave? After all, she'd held up her end of the bargain—leaving her home, moving in with him, completing the paperwork to change their son's last name—and the one thing he'd promised her, he couldn't come through on.

I lowered my personal standards to become the plaything of a man who deemed me good enough for a fuck but not to escort past the kitchen. Every time I wear that necklace it's a reminder to myself to never repeat that mistake.

He locked his knees, steadying himself as Charlotte's words threatened to knock him back into the chair. Yes, they'd disappeared during the event and had sex. And later that night, after they returned home, he'd lost himself in her again. But he couldn't eject those words from his head. Couldn't convince himself that, although she'd apologized, she hadn't meant them.

She'd called him a mistake and it was nothing he hadn't thought before. A mistake to her, to his parents, even to the women he'd fucked and forgotten. Which made sense in a screwed-up but logical way. Because if he was truly important to them, how could they so easily walk away from him?

So while he'd had Charlotte's body, he didn't have her loyalty. Definitely not her love, not that he'd asked for that, and not since she'd made it clear he was an error she'd never repeat. The bottom line was he had no hold on her, except their son, that would compel her to stay with him. And Charlotte had proven her capability in raising Ben as a single parent.

No.

The objection blasted through his head, loud and furious. Ben was his son. And regardless of whether she left or not, he wouldn't allow her to take Ben away from him.

"Don't worry, Dad," Ross said, arching an eyebrow and forcing an indifference that was a lie. "I won't come crawling back. And I'll make sure to use you as an example. Both you and Sarabeth."

With that, he spun on his heel and left Rusty's office. His every good intention in this visit had backfired. But he'd emerged crystal clear on one thing.

He couldn't count on his father to be there.

Couldn't depend on Charlotte, either.

The only person who would never fail him was himself.

Fourteen

Charlotte sighed, sliding the key into the front door. Usually, Mondays were a slow night, but for some reason, it seemed as if every person in Royal had decided to drop by Sheen tonight. Jeremy had credited the unprecedented influx with her presence at the Soiree on the Bay fundraising event over the weekend as well as the samples of their dishes. Possibly. She'd shared his opinion with Ross when he'd brought Ben by the restaurant to see her, and he'd managed not to throw an "I told you so" at her.

She frowned, unlocking the door and twisting the knob. Actually, Ross had been distant and aloof tonight. Since Saturday, they'd formed a tenuous truce, but he'd reverted to being that cold, reserved man she'd met at Sheen weeks ago. A tight ball of dread had settled in the pit of her stomach and remained there for the rest of the evening like a pebble she couldn't shake from her shoe. It had been a relief when the night ended, because she'd come to a decision sometime between preparing the sauce for her signature dish and plating dishes for a party of twelve—she needed to be honest with Ross.

She had to tell him that as hard as she'd tried, as angry as she'd been, she'd never stopped loving him.

Fear trickled through her as she entered the house. But intertwined with those dark tendrils was excitement, too. He'd been jealous, possessive on Saturday. And there was no denying he'd been hurt by her. That had to mean he felt *something* more for her than he would for a tolerable person to co-parent with… God, she hoped so. Because she'd been here before, three years ago. Uncertain. Scared. Hopeful.

Only to end up broken, devastated and alone.

Would she survive that kind of agony again?

Would she have to?

It was those two questions that had her wavering back and forth. She didn't know if her heart could stand losing him again…but what if she didn't lose him?

That damn hope. It was both a blessing and a curse.

Still, she couldn't just continue to exist in this torturous limbo. Tonight, she'd have her answer. Tonight, she'd—

"Dammit." She stumbled to a halt, her toe throbbing in protest at whatever she'd just stubbed it on. Frowning, she glanced down. "What the hell?" she murmured, spotting the set of black luggage in the foyer. The smallest of the two listed to the side from the kick she'd inadvertently delivered to it.

"Charlotte, I need to speak to you."

She shifted her gaze from the suitcases to Ross, who stood just inside the entryway to the living room. It was a little after twelve, and most nights when she arrived home, worn jeans or loose-fitting sleep pants adorned his tall frame. But tonight, a dark gray suit had replaced the pajamas and T-shirt.

Her frown deepened. "Hey." She set her bag and purse down on the table beside the door. "Did I forget you had a business trip or were headed out of town?"

"No," he said, both his voice and face shuttered. That knot in her stomach pulled taut, and dread crept inside her, an unwelcome intruder. "Can we talk in here?"

He turned, but she didn't move. "No," she whispered. He halted and slowly pivoted back to face her, and she shook her head. "No," she repeated, stronger, louder. "Whatever you have to say, we can do it right here. Especially since you'll be leaving directly afterward, right?" His expression remained a mask of stone, but she caught the flicker in his eyes, and she let loose a low, jagged chuckle that abraded her throat. A heavy, suffocating weight settled on her chest, shortening her breath, causing an echo in her ears. She recognized this feeling. The forerunner of panic, of an onslaught of fear. But she shoved it back, focusing on the silent, brooding and cruelly beautiful man before her. "Let's just get this over with so you have easy access to the door."

"Fine." He nodded, sliding his hands into the front pockets of his suit. How could he be so cold? So unfeeling when she was shattering into pieces? "I haven't been honest with you. After a meeting with my financial advisor, I can't afford to pay you the half-million dollars that I promised. It wouldn't be fair of me to expect you to hold up your end of our agreement when I can't. Of course, you and Ben can continue to stay here—"

"Liar."

Ross's head jerked back as if her accusation had delivered a verbal punch.

"I never asked for that money in the first place, so don't try to place the blame for you leaving on it. You saw your father today, didn't you?"

"I don't know how you found out about it—and not that it matters—but, yes," he said, eyes narrowing on her.

"Gina called me because she was trying to get in touch with you, and you weren't answering your phone. Apparently, your father was on the warpath today because you showed up at the office. She wanted to make sure you were okay." Charlotte shook her head, a bone-deep weariness and ache invading her. "And to think I felt that this time, maybe, just maybe, things would be different."

Ross sliced a hand through the air. "I don't know what conclusions you've drawn in your head, Charlotte, but like I said, this has nothing to do with Rusty. I'm trying to do what's right here. What's fair."

"I don't know if you truly believe that or if you're really trying to convince yourself of it." She wrapped her arms around herself. "When I left for California, I so desperately wanted you to fight for me. To ask me to stay. To stand up to your father and tell him you and I were together and nothing he could do would change your mind. But you didn't. And I resented you for a long time because of it. But this time, you did exactly that. Maybe not for me, but for Ben. Still, you defied Rusty, and it made me hopeful. It made me foolish," she added with a self-deprecating chuckle. "Because all it took was one visit with Rusty and you fell right back in line. Same result, just took a bit longer."

"That's bullshit," he snapped, eyes bright with anger. "I'm not abandoning you or Ben. I still want joint custody. Or are you trying to tell me that because I don't want to live in this house, I can't continue to see my son on a regular basis? Because I won't allow you to cut me out of his life."

"Wow," she whispered. "For a moment, I could've sworn Rusty Edmond stood before me instead of Ross." He flinched, paling at her direct hit, but she didn't back down. "Contrary to whatever nonsense your father might've spouted about me only wanting you for your money and withholding Ben to get it, I would never do that to Ben. He adores you. But I'd also never do that to you."

She tunneled her fingers through her hair and briefly closed her eyes. Ordering herself not to shed one damn tear in front of him. He didn't deserve to see her pain. "You just don't get it, Ross," she rasped. "Three years ago, I fell in love with you. You. An Edmond. A man I should've run far away from. But I couldn't, because under the bravado was a unique, vulnerable, funny, sweet, *good* man who made me feel more special than I'd ever felt in my life. You weren't your father, no matter how hard Rusty tried to make you conform to be the image of him. And I loved that about you."

"You never said…" Ross stared at her, eyes dark with surprise, body unnaturally stiff. "Why didn't you…"

"Because you didn't want that from me. I knew what I was to you even if I hoped for different. Your father would never accept me, and when you surrendered to that and ended things with me because Rusty didn't see me as worthy enough, I knew it would break me. So I left before it could happen. I ran from here, but I couldn't outrun my heart. And then I found out I was pregnant. I accepted then, even after the phone call and letter, that you would always be a part of me. So when you appeared back in my life, in Ben's life, I convinced myself I could be happy with our co-parenting-with-benefits arrangement. But I lied. That's what I planned to tell you tonight. I want all of you or nothing. Seems like you'd already made that decision for both of us, though."

Not giving him a chance to reply—because really, what could he say when he literally had his bags packed?—she crossed the foyer for the staircase. But she paused at the bottom step, hand on the newel.

She didn't look at him as she offered him one last confession.

"Do you remember when you gave me the diamond heart necklace?" she murmured. "You'd taken me to the resort on Appaloosa Island, and one night after making love, you surprised me with it. You'd bought it at one of the shops because it reminded you of me. You said the heart reminded you of mine—beautiful and precious. That's why I kept the necklace, Ross. Because of all the gifts you'd given me, this one meant the most. No motive behind it. You bought it simply because you'd been thinking of me. And my heart."

She climbed the steps and didn't look back.

Fifteen

"Ross? A word."

Ross froze at his father's request. Request, hell. Rusty had issued the order and expected to be obeyed. He glanced at the door to the meeting room, debating whether he wanted to give his father the "word" he wanted. But in the end, he remained in place, curiosity momentarily overriding animosity and bitterness.

"You okay?" Asher murmured, pausing beside him. His brother, sister, Billy and Rusty had met at the clubhouse for a meeting about the festival, since Ross refused to return to the family's office building. He wasn't a fan of going where he wasn't wanted. "I can stay."

"No," Ross said, studying Rusty's face as his father tossed Asher an irritated glance. "I'm fine. I'll call you later."

His brother clapped him on the shoulder, and Gina squeezed his hand as she passed by him. Billy patted him on the back, and then moments later, the door closed, leaving him alone with his father.

"What's this about?" Ross asked, crossing his arms.

Rusty took his time answering, rounding the table and hiking a hip on the edge of it. For several long moments, he studied Ross, and he steadily met his father's stare. If Rusty expected him to fidget like a kid called on the carpet, then he'd have a long wait.

"I heard you're no longer shacking up with that woman and her kid," his father finally said, the smug note in his voice raking over Ross's skin.

"I have to commend the Royal grapevine," Ross drawled. "It's only been three days."

Three interminable, hollow, gray days since he'd walked out of the Pine Valley home he'd bought for his family. Three days since he'd woken up to Ben's laughter and demands for banana pancakes.

Three days since he'd last seen Charlotte. Heard her voice. Inhaled her scent. Touched her body.

He clenched his jaw, fisting the hands in his pockets.

Three days since she'd lobbed her bomb about being in love with him years ago and wanting all of him now.

It was also that long since he'd been able to draw a breath that didn't have razors attached to it. God, why couldn't he carve this Charlotte-sized ache out of his chest? Evict her voice from his head? Only working on the various projects he'd thrown himself into had kept him sane. The projects and Ben.

"News like that travels fast, son," Rusty said.

"I'm *son* now?" Ross chuckled. "Since when? Let me guess. Three days ago."

"You did the right thing, Ross." Rusty nodded, mouth flattening into a grim line. "I hate that I had to take such drastic measures to make you see what a mistake you were making, but if the end result was you coming to your senses, then I'll live with my actions. You deserve someone who adds to your wealth, social standing and reputation, not some faithless, disloyal *cook*," he sneered. "Just tell me the situation has been handled and we can move on from here."

Ross stared at Rusty, shocked by the venom that seemed directed at Charlotte. Yes, she'd been their employee, but she was also a successful, gifted chef. What the hell had she ever done to deserve Rusty's enmity?

He slashed a hand through the air. Fuck it. His father took classism and snobbery to a whole new level, but he was through allowing his father to run his life like it was one of his subsidiaries.

"Is that what you assumed? That I left Charlotte because of you disinheriting me?" He shook his head, his bark of laughter drawing a fierce frown from his father. "Sorry, Dad, but I regret to inform you that I'm still as much of a disappointment as I was when I left your office. This has nothing to do with you. It was my choice because I was trying to do what was best for her. And Charlotte and Ben aren't a *situation* to be *handled*," he snapped. "He's my son, and she's the mother of my son. She and I aren't living together—" weren't together *at all* "—but I'm not abandoning my son. So your praise might've been a tad premature."

Rusty slid off the edge of the table, standing to his

full, intimidating height. Well, it used to be intimidating. Not any longer. Somewhere between watching Charlotte strip herself emotionally bare before walking away and leaving him broken, and checking into The Bellamy, his father's approval and acceptance had stopped being the driving force in his life. There were only two people whose esteem mattered. One loved him unconditionally. And the other? Well, the other, he'd hurt so badly that there was no coming back from it.

"Ross, I don't know what this is, but you need to get your shit together," Rusty thundered. "You will not have any association with that woman or child. This is nonnegotiable."

Ross studied his father as if it were the first time he was truly seeing him. "You want me to choose you over Charlotte, over my son. Which is so damn ironic because in every situation you never offered me the same courtesy. Business first. Women first. Yourself first. But never me, my happiness, my well-being. No," he stated flatly, with a finality that resonated through him. "I won't do it. Keep your money, your inheritance, your business empire. And if you're stubborn enough to demand it, your title as my father. When my son looks at me with love and respect, knowing I'll always be there for him, that's worth more than anything you could possibly hold over my head. Goodbye, Dad."

He turned and strode toward the door, the crushing weight of guilt, sadness and anger on his chest a little bit lighter.

"Don't you walk away from me, Ross. We're not finished here," Rusty bellowed. Like a child throwing a temper tantrum.

"Yes, Dad, we are."

He opened the door, stepped through and closed it behind him.

Closing it on his past.

Ross handed his car keys to The Bellamy's valet and entered the hotel's entrance. His cell phone jangled in his pocket, and like the last three times his sister had called since he'd left his confrontation with Rusty, he ignored it. He loved Gina, but right now his emotions huddled too close to the surface. They were too raw, and he couldn't hold a conversation with her.

He strode across the lobby toward the elevators, but as he passed the sitting area, a woman rose from one of the chairs. Shock barreled into him, jerking him to a sudden halt.

No. Not today. All the anger, pain and sadness simmering inside him ratcheted to a boil and flowed over him, singing him with memories, bitterness and a little boy's betrayal and love.

"Sarabeth."

His mother's smile wavered but then rallied. Probably all that beauty pageant training. Oh, how Rusty used to go on about that. How he'd found her on the pageant circuit and lifted her out of her lower-middle-class life to rarefied Royal society. And all he'd received in return was a coldhearted gold digger more concerned with what he could do for her, instead of the wife and mother he'd wanted.

Ross hadn't cared about any of that at the time. At ten, all he'd wanted was his mother.

He studied the tall, willowy blonde as she approached

him. Though nearing fifty years old, his mother appeared ten or fifteen years younger. All that free living without the baggage of children could do that to a
person, he mused.

"Ross, I'm sorry to ambush you like this," Sarabeth
apologized, the blue eyes he'd inherited from her meeting his. She chuckled, and it struck him as nervous. Of
course, cornering the son she hadn't seen or talked to
in years had to be stressful. "God, in some ways you
look exactly the same. I would've recognized you anywhere." When he didn't reply to that, she shook her
head, that smile finally fading. "I understand if you'd
rather not see me, but if you could give me just a few
minutes, I'd really appreciate it."

He smothered his initial instinct to tell her no, and
dipped his chin. Pivoting on his heel, he stalked toward
The Silver Saddle, trusting her to follow. At two o'clock,
most of the tables remained empty, a stark contrast to
how it would be jumping with patrons in just three
more hours. But for now, he snagged one in a corner
that would afford them privacy.

Once they were seated and had placed their orders
with their waitress—a beer for him and a white wine
for her—she folded her slim hands on the table and
gazed at him.

"I'm sorry for staring," she apologized after an awkward silence. "It's just that… It's been a long time. I've
missed you."

"I've been in the same town, at the same address
all this time," he said brusquely. "If you missed me so
much, you knew where to find me."

"I deserve that," she whispered, hooking a strand of

hair behind her ear. "There's so much I want to say to you…" She cleared her throat, momentarily dropping her eyes to the table before lifting them to him. "Will you hear me out? Please? And at the end if you still want to walk out of here and have nothing to do with me, then I'll understand."

"Fine." He leaned back in his chair as the waitress set their drinks on the table. Twisting the cap off his beer, he tipped it toward her. "I'm listening."

"Thank you." Her inhale of breath echoed between them, as did the long exhale. "I want to preface this by saying I'm not excusing my absence from your life. I just want to explain my side of it and hope that maybe you can forgive me."

She sipped from her wineglass. For courage? Because that was the reason he gulped down his beer. To try to bolster the bravado to sit here and listen to his mother explain why he hadn't been important enough for her to stay in his life.

"I married your father when I was young—nineteen. Like a fairy tale, he whisked me away to this beautiful home, provided a life I'd only dreamed about. I guess you could say Rusty pampered me, because he did. Beautiful children, a home, clothes, jewelry, cars, vacations abroad—everything I could ever ask for. Except for a faithful husband."

She lifted her glass for another sip, this one a little longer than her last. And when she lowered her arm, her slim fingers slightly trembled around the long stem.

"I couldn't stay in a loveless marriage any longer," she continued, her voice a shade huskier. "Not when I walked in on Rusty with another woman. Asking him for a divorce was terrifying, but at least I had you and your sister. Or at least, I naively believed. As punishment for daring to leave him, Rusty used all his power, including a judge who knew him, to ensure he got custody of you and Gina. I might have received a financial settlement, but what mattered most to me—my children—I lost."

Ross tried to steel his heart against her tale; he'd heard some of it through Rusty. But the cheating, the judge in Rusty's pocket? No, his father had left those details out. Not that either shocked him. When Rusty played to win, he refused to lose at all costs.

Still, she'd left his father. Why had she then divorced her children?

As if she read his mind, she continued, her voice low, pained, "I tried to maintain a relationship with you and Gina. God, I tried. But you two were growing older and preferred to be with your friends rather than a woman who was increasingly becoming a stranger to you. I got it. And Rusty didn't help matters, either. He didn't try to enforce our custody arrangement. Then I couldn't find work here in Royal, and everyone treated me like the scorned ex-wife. I had to leave town simply to survive."

As someone who'd recently been on the receiving end of Rusty's hardhanded tactics, an unprecedented empathy he'd never offered his mother swelled within him. He understood survival.

He understood trying to escape the steel, booby-trapped box Rusty could trap a person in.

"Now, in hindsight, I wish I'd fought harder to get you back. To try another court if one didn't listen. The Edmond name and power extends beyond Royal, and

I didn't have the financial resources to fight. But if I'd known divorcing him would mean losing you and your sister, I would've stayed married to him, regardless of his mistreatment and cheating."

She stretched her arms across the table, hesitated, but then carefully clasped his hands in hers. "Ross, I have so many regrets. And the main one is allowing fear of your rejection to keep me from reaching out to you in all this time. As your mother, it was up to me to connect with you, not place that burden on you. I just ask for your forgiveness." A tear slipped down her cheek, and she swiped at it before clasping his hand again. "Like I said, I have many regrets. But in spite of the hell I went through with your father, I'd do it again in a heartbeat, because it brought me you and Gina."

A quaking started in Ross's chest, and then a loud crack he was surprised no one could hear crashed in his head and through his heart. He was so damn tired of being bitter. It had eaten away at him for so long that sometimes he didn't recognize the man he'd become. He'd been punishing everyone because of this anger—his father, Charlotte, himself.

God, *Charlotte*.

Three years ago, he hadn't allowed himself to love her because he'd been so afraid she would leave him. And when she had, it had been a self-fulfilling prophecy. Then, after she'd come back in his life, offering him a second chance with her, a chance to have a family, he'd again fallen back on fear. Walking out on her before she could.

He was tired of being afraid. Tired of being bitter and angry.

He just wanted to be loved, to be…happy.

He blinked against the sting of tears as he stared at the woman he'd always just wanted to love him, to accept him.

To stay for him.

Maybe she hadn't then, but she was here now.

Just as Charlotte had wanted to be.

Oh, Christ, he'd screwed up so bad. So *goddamn* bad. But he could start fixing it now. And that healing had to start with Sarabeth—with his mother.

"I've blamed a lot of my actions and behavior on you and your leaving me. I've hurt the mother of my son, the woman I…love—" his throat closed around the word, at admitting it for the first time aloud "—because I couldn't grow up and accept accountability. I'm sorry for all that you went through, and that when I was old enough, I chose to wallow in resentment than ask you why. I needed you when I was younger, and you weren't there. So I can't say that I can magically let go of that hurt, but I do forgive you. Because forgiving you means forgiving myself."

"Oh, honey," Sarabeth whispered, more tears streaming down her face. She cupped his cheek, and he savored it. Cherished the affection from his mom that he'd craved for so long. "I can't make up for the past. If only I could. But if you'll let me, I'll be here for you now. And the woman you love? Don't make the same mistakes I did, Ross. Go after her. Fight for her."

I so desperately wanted you to fight for me. To ask me to stay.

Charlotte's voice echoed in his head, and he silently vowed that he wouldn't fail her now like he had in the past.

He would go to war for both her and Ben, and this was one he couldn't lose.

Because he was battling for the woman he loved and his child.

He was battling for his life.

Sixteen

"I need the braised beef," Charlotte called out from the warming shelves as she finished plating a Tomahawk steak entrée. "It's up next."

"Yes, Chef, on two," her sous-chef replied.

Satisfied, Charlotte returned to the dishes waiting for her to check and send out. Sheen had been packed since the Soiree on the Bay party, and this Friday night, they had a line out the building, of customers waiting to dine. The knowledge should've filled her with happiness at their success, but for the past week—since Ross had left—everything had been shrouded in a layer of gray, dulling her emotions. Which she appreciated. Because she feared feeling *anything*. Feared that if she allowed even a sliver to surface, then the pain, disappointment and grief would surge through that opening like scavengers, to feed on her.

No, this coat of numbness was saving her at the moment, and she clung to it.

"Chef, you have a guest who'd like to see you tableside."

Dammit.

Forcing a smile that probably resembled a grimace, Charlotte glanced over at Carlie, who stood in the kitchen doorway.

"Okay, I'll be out in just a minute."

Switching out her jackets, she hurried from the kitchen with instructions to her sous-chef to take over for her. The sooner she got this over with, the quicker she could return to the kitchen, her sanctuary. Where she could lose herself in work and think about nothing else. No *one* else.

"Right over here, Chef," Carlie said, guiding her toward the back of the restaurant.

Charlotte followed, threading through the tables, pausing to greet diners but steadily moving forward. Hopefully, this guest wasn't chatty. She couldn't abide a talker right now...

"Hello, Charlotte."

She slammed to a halt, the air pummeling from her lungs at the sight of the man who hadn't left her mind in a week. Her knees locked, preventing her from crumbling to the floor. What the hell? Why was Ross here?

She glanced at Carlie, but the server had already disappeared. There had to be some mistake...

"No mistake," Ross murmured, because she'd obviously said the thought aloud. He rose from his chair, his tall frame towering over her. Reminding her of how well his body sheltered her.

No. *Hell no.* Not going there.

"What are you doing here, Ross?" she rasped. God, the gazes on them crawled under her jacket, skating over her skin. She *hated* it. No doubt this little visit would be the new topic of gossip.

"I came to see you." As if that were enough explanation. He cocked his head, his blue eyes gleaming with… what? Nope, she didn't care. "You look beautiful."

"Seriously?" she hissed. "After walking out of our house, leaving a home you bought for a family you claimed you wanted, that's what you come to my place of business to tell me?" She glared at him. "I don't know what game you're playing, but I quit."

"No game, baby," he murmured, causing her heart to shudder and twist at the endearment. He had *no* right to call her that. None. "I forfeited my privilege to come and go in the house, so I didn't want to ambush you there. Because that's what this is. An ambush. I freely admit that."

"What? You don't believe I'll cause a scene and kick you out of the restaurant with all these witnesses?" He was correct, damn him. But he didn't have to know that.

"I hoped you wouldn't," he said. Sighing, he threaded his fingers through his hair, disheveling the thick strands. That gesture of nerves from him, especially in front of a restaurant full of people took her aback. Again, what the hell was going on? "Two minutes, Charlotte. Can you give me two minutes?"

He lifted his arm, and it hovered between them for an instant before he gently brushed the back of his fingers down her cheek. A gasp lodged in her throat, and she stiffened, despising her body's programmed response.

Lush desire flowed through her, as if only needing his touch to once again stir to life.

She stepped back.

His head dipped in a nod, his eyes dimming. "I came here to apologize, to *beg* if I have to, for your forgiveness. I don't deserve it, but it's not stopping me from asking for it. Charlotte—" he held his hands up in the age-old sign of surrender "—I walked away for one reason. I was terrified of losing you. I figured I'd do it first before you could do it to me. Because I believed you eventually would. Whether it was in a week, a month or when the year was up, you would leave. Especially after I was disinherited and didn't even have wealth or connections to offer you." His mouth twisted, but the disgust in it seemed self-directed. "I was so fucking scared to let you in that I convinced myself it was better to end things sooner before I became used to a life with you and Ben. Before I let myself believe the idea of having both of you could be forever. Before I fell in love with you. But it was too late. I'd fallen back in love with you the moment you approached this table weeks ago. I was just too much of a stubborn coward to admit it."

He balled his fingers into fists and stared down at them. "I was so determined to hold on to the past—of you leaving me years ago, of missing that time with Ben, of not believing you could possibly want me for myself—that I lost my future. And if that's true, if you can't forgive me, then that's on me, and I'll have to live with it. But I can't let another moment go by with you not knowing that I love you. I've never loved any other woman *but* you. For three years, you've haunted me, never left me. And finally, having you back, it's a miracle that I callously threw away."

"Ross," she whispered, stunned speechless. Pressing her hands to her chest, she stared at him, afraid to trust. Afraid to take that step toward him.

Afraid he would devastate her again.

"I broke us, baby," he said. Swallowing hard, he paused, then shifted forward, claiming the space she'd placed between them. "I'm begging for the chance to put us back together. Let me prove to you that I am the man you need. Let me give you and Ben my last name. Let me love you. I don't need an inheritance if I have you and Ben. You're all I need. And, baby, I do need you."

Pride could have her reject him in front of all these people. Teach him a lesson. But she didn't care about other people. Didn't care about punishing him. Punishing them.

All she cared about was *him*.

She loved him.

"I never cared about your money," she said, meeting his bright gaze. "I was in love with the man—still am in love with him. If you come to us penniless, it's okay. You and Ben… If I have you two, I have everything."

"Baby," he breathed, then lunged forward, cupping her face, tipping it back and taking her mouth in a blistering kiss that leveled her. Pulling back, he pressed his forehead to hers, swiping his thumbs over her cheeks. "There's so much I have to tell you. Will you sit with me? Have dinner with me?"

"I wish I could—"

He chuckled, brushing another kiss over her lips. "On the hope that you would give me another chance,

I cleared it with Jeremy for you to take a break from the kitchen and have a romantic dinner with me."

"Well, didn't you think of everything?" She grinned, and stepping back, encircled his wrist and led him back to the table. "I would love to."

Once they were seated, Carlie appeared with a wide grin and set down two plates of her signature dish before Charlotte and Ross.

"You'll never believe what happened…"

Over dinner, Ross told her about the confrontation with his father and the surprise visit from his mother. She held his hand as he relayed how they tentatively started the process of healing their relationship, which had culminated in Sarabeth urging Ross to go after Charlotte.

"Wow. I owe your mother a debt of gratitude for her advice," she said, caressing the back of his hand. "I'm sorry I didn't have the opportunity to meet her."

"She's actually planning to move back to Royal so she can get to know her new grandson." He smiled, and joy for him burned like the sun in her heart.

"That's amazing, Ross." She straightened in her chair and exhaled a breath, keeping a hold of his hand. If they were going to start their relationship anew, then he deserved the whole truth. It was time for it. "I don't want to begin our foundation on secrets, so I have something to tell you. I haven't been completely honest about why I left three years ago." God, she didn't want to hurt him. "Rusty had started hitting on me."

Anger darkened Ross's face, his narrowed eyes flaring bright.

"Did he touch you?" he growled.

"No," she assured him, even as she almost sagged in

her chair. Because he believed her. That had been one of her fears back then. But he accepted her word as truth. If possible, she loved him more. "He didn't get physical, but he was insistent, and I grew uncomfortable. Especially with us being involved and knowing the power Rusty wielded. I didn't tell you earlier because you love your father, and a relationship with him was important to you. And I didn't want to taint that in any way. But if we're starting over, we need a clean slate. No secrets. And also—" she briefly closed her eyes before meeting his unwavering gaze "—I want to apologize for putting all the blame on you for leaving back then. I had a part in it. And not just because of Rusty and his connections. I was afraid that if we went public, you would see how others looked at us together and not want me anymore. That had nothing to do with you and everything to do with my own sense of self-esteem."

"Baby, you have nothing to apologize for. Nothing at all." He stood, rounded the table and gently pulled her from her seat. Cradling her cheek, he smiled, his love for her so brilliant she would never doubt it again. "Right here, right now, is where we begin. The past is over with and you are my future. I need you, Charlotte Jarrett-soon-to-be-Edmond. I love you."

She turned into his palm, placing a tender kiss to the center. "I love you, too, Ross. You've always been my forever. You always will be."

* * * * *

Don't miss the next book in the
Texas Cattleman's Club: Heir Apparent series,
available March 2021!

At the Rancher's Pleasure
by Joss Wood

Runaway groom Brett Harrison was Royal's
favorite topic until Sarabeth Edmonds returned.
Banished years before by her ex-husband, she's
determined to reclaim her life and reputation.
But a spontaneous kiss meant to rile up town gossips
unleashes a passionate romance neither can ignore...

SPECIAL EXCERPT FROM

(H)HARLEQUIN
DESIRE

When a scandal jeopardizes playboy CEO Drew Maddox's career, he proposes a fake engagement to his brilliant and philanthropic friend Jenna Sommers to revitalize his reputation and fund her efforts. But as passion takes over, can this bad boy reform his ways for her?

Read on for a sneak peek at
His Perfect Fake Engagement
by New York Times *bestselling author Shannon McKenna!*

Drew pulled her toward the big Mercedes SUV idling at the curb. "Here's your ride," he said. "We still on for tonight? I wouldn't blame you if you changed your mind. The paparazzi are a huge pain in the ass. Like a weather condition. Or a zombie horde."

"I'm still game," she said. "Let `em do their worst."

That got her a smile that touched off fireworks at every level of her consciousness.

For God's sake. Get a grip, girl.

"I'll pick you up for dinner at eight fifteen," he said. "Our reservation at Peccati di Gola is at eight forty-five."

"I'll be ready," she promised.

"Can I put my number into your phone, so you can text me your address?"

"Of course." She handed him her phone and waited as he tapped the number into it. He hit Call and waited for the ring.

"There," she said, taking her phone back. "You've got me now."

"Lucky me," he murmured. He glanced back at the photographers, still blocked by three security men at the door, still snapping photos. "You're no delicate flower, are you?"

"By no means," she assured him.

"I like that," he said. He'd already opened the car door for her, but as she was about to get inside, he pulled her swiftly back up again and covered her mouth with his.

His kiss was hotter than the last one. Deliberate, demanding. He pressed her closer, tasting her lips.

Oh. Wow. He tasted amazing. Like fire, like wind. Like sunlight on the ocean. She dug her fingers into the massive bulk of his shoulders, or tried to. He was so thick and solid. Her fingers slid helplessly over the fabric of his jacket. They could get no grip.

His lips parted hers. The tip of his tongue flicked against hers, coaxed her to open, to give herself up. To yield to him. His kiss promised infinite pleasure in return. It demanded surrender on a level so deep and primal, she responded instinctively.

She melted against him with a shudder of emotion that was absolutely unfaked.

Holy crap. Panic pierced her as she realized what was happening. He'd kissed her like he meant it, and she'd responded in the same way. As naturally as breathing.

She was so screwed.

Jenna pulled away, shaking. She felt like a mask had been pulled off. That he could see straight into the depths of her most private self.

And Drew helped her into the car and gave her a reassuring smile and a friendly wave as the car pulled away, like it was no big deal. As if he hadn't just tongue-kissed her passionately in front of a crowd of photographers and caused an inner earthquake.

Her lips were still glowing. They tingled from the contact.

She couldn't let her mind stray down this path. She was a means to an end.

It was Drew Maddox's nature to be seductive. He was probably that way with every woman he talked to. He probably couldn't help himself. Not even if he tried.

She had to keep that fact firmly in mind.

All. The. Time.

Don't miss what happens next in...
His Perfect Fake Engagement
by New York Times *bestselling author Shannon McKenna!*

Available March 2021 wherever
Harlequin Desire books and ebooks are sold.

Harlequin.com